THE COUNTRY OF THE BLIND

And Other Stories

H. G. WELLS

[Illustration: He stopped, and then made a dash to escape from their closing ranks.]

INTRODUCTION

The enterprise of Messrs. T. Nelson & Sons and the friendly accommodation of Messrs. Macmillan render possible this collection in one cover of all the short stories by me that I care for any one to read again. Except for the two series of linked incidents that make up the bulk of the book called Tales of Space and Time, no short story of mine of the slightest merit is excluded from this volume. Many of very questionable merit find a place; it is an inclusive and not an exclusive gathering. And the task of selection and revision brings home to me with something of the effect of discovery that I was once an industrious writer of short stories, and that I am no longer anything of the kind. I have not written one now for quite a long time, and in the past five or six years I have made scarcely one a year. The bulk of the fifty or sixty tales from which this present three-and-thirty have been chosen dates from the last century. This edition is more definitive than I supposed when first I arranged for it. In the presence of so conclusive an ebb and cessation an almost obituary manner seems justifiable.

I find it a little difficult to disentangle the causes that have restricted the flow of these inventions. It has happened, I remark, to others as well as to myself, and in spite of the kindliest encouragement to continue from editors and readers. There was a time when life bubbled with short stories; they were always coming to the surface of my mind, and it is no deliberate change of will that has thus restricted my production. It is rather, I think, a diversion of attention to more sustained and more exacting forms. It was my friend Mr. C.L. Hind who set that spring going. He urged me to write short stories for the Pall Mall Budget, and persuaded me by his simple and buoyant conviction that I could do what he desired. There existed at the time only the little sketch, "The Jilting of Jane," included in this volume—at least, that is the only tolerable fragment of fiction I find surviving from my pre-Lewis-Hind period. But I set myself, so encouraged, to the experiment of inventing moving and interesting things that could be given vividly in the little space of eight or ten such pages as this, and for a time I found it a very entertaining pursuit indeed. Mr. Hind's indicating finger had shown me an amusing possibility of the mind. I found that, taking almost anything as a starting-point and letting my thoughts play about it, there would presently come out of the darkness, in a manner quite inexplicable, some absurd or vivid little incident more or less relevant to that initial nucleus. Little men in canoes upon sunlit oceans would come floating out of nothingness, incubating the eggs of prehistoric monsters unawares; violent conflicts would break out amidst the flower-beds of suburban gardens; I would discover I was peering into remote and mysterious worlds ruled by an order logical indeed but other than our common sanity.

The 'nineties was a good and stimulating period for a short-story writer. Mr. Kipling had made his astonishing advent with a series of little blue-grey books, whose covers opened like window-shutters to reveal the dusty sun-glare and blazing colours of the East; Mr. Barrie had demonstrated what could be done in a little space through the panes of his Window in Thrums. The National Observer was at the climax of its career of heroic insistence upon lyrical brevity and a vivid finish, and Mr. Frank Harris was not only printing good short stories by other people, but writing still better ones himself in the dignified pages of the Fortnightly Review. Longman's Magazine, too, represented a clientèle of appreciative short-story readers that is now scattered. Then came the generous opportunities of the Yellow Book, and the National Observer died only to give birth to the New Review. No short story of the slightest distinction went for long unrecognised. The sixpenny popular magazines had still to deaden down the conception of what a short story might be to the imaginative limitation of the common reader—and a maximum length of six thousand words. Short stories broke out everywhere. Kipling was writing short stories; Barrie, Stevenson, Frank-Harris; Max Beerbohm wrote at least one perfect one, "The Happy Hypocrite"; Henry James pursued his wonderful and inimitable bent; and among other names that occur to me, like a mixed handful of jewels drawn from a bag, are George Street, Morley Roberts, George Gissing, Ella d'Arcy, Murray Gilchrist, E. Nesbit, Stephen Crane, Joseph Conrad, Edwin Pugh, Jerome K. Jerome, Kenneth Graham, Arthur Morrison, Marriott Watson, George Moore, Grant Allen, George Egerton, Henry Harland, Pett Ridge, W. W. Jacobs (who alone seems inexhaustible). I dare say I could recall as many more names with a little effort. I may be succumbing to the infirmities of middle age, but I do not think the present decade can produce any parallel to this list, or what is more remarkable, that the later achievements in this field of any of the survivors from that time, with the sole exception of Joseph Conrad, can compare with the work they did before 1900. It seems to me this outburst of short stories came not only as a phase in literary development, but also as a phase in the development of the individual writers concerned.

It is now quite unusual to see any adequate criticism of short stories in English. I do not know how far the decline in short-story writing may not be due to that. Every sort of artist demands human responses, and few men can contrive to write merely for a publisher's cheque and silence, however reassuring that cheque may be. A mad millionaire who commissioned masterpieces to burn would find it impossible to buy them. Scarcely any artist will hesitate in the choice between money and attention; and it was primarily for that last and better sort of pay that the short stories of the 'nineties were written. People talked about them tremendously, compared them, and ranked them. That was the thing that mattered.

It was not, of course, all good talk, and we suffered then, as now, from the à priori critic. Just as nowadays he goes about declaring that the work of such-and-such a dramatist is all very amusing and delightful, but "it isn't a Play," so we' had a great deal of talk about the short story, and found ourselves measured by all kinds of arbitrary standards. There was a tendency to treat the short story as though it was as definable a form as the sonnet, instead of being just exactly what any one of courage and imagination can get told in twenty minutes' reading or so. It was either Mr. Edward Garnett or Mr. George Moore in a violently anti-Kipling mood who invented the distinction between the short story and the anecdote. The short story was Maupassant; the anecdote was damnable. It was a quite infernal comment in its way, because it permitted no defence. Fools caught it up and used it freely. Nothing is so destructive in a field of artistic effort as a stock term of abuse. Anyone could say of any short story, "A mere anecdote," just as anyone can say "Incoherent!" of any novel or of any sonata that isn't studiously monotonous. The recession of enthusiasm for this compact, amusing form is closely associated in my mind with that discouraging imputation. One felt hopelessly open to a paralysing and unanswerable charge, and one's ease and happiness in the garden of one's fancies was more and more marred by the dread of it. It crept into one's mind, a distress as vague and inexpugnable as a sea fog on a spring morning, and presently one shivered and wanted to go indoors...It is the absurd fate of the imaginative writer that he should be thus sensitive to atmospheric conditions.

But after one has died as a maker one may still live as a critic, and I will confess I am all for laxness and variety in this as in every field of art. Insistence upon rigid forms and austere unities seems to me the instinctive reaction of the sterile against the fecund. It is the tired man with a headache who values a work of art for what it does not contain. I suppose it is the lot of every critic nowadays to suffer from indigestion and a fatigued appreciation, and to develop a self-protective tendency towards rules that will reject, as it were, automatically the more abundant and irregular forms. But this world is not for the weary, and in the long-run it is the new and variant that matter. I refuse altogether to recognise any hard and fast type for the Short Story, any more than I admit any limitation upon the liberties of the Small Picture. The short story is a fiction that may be read in something under an hour, and so that it is moving and delightful, it does not matter whether it is as "trivial" as a Japanese print of insects seen closely between grass stems, or as spacious as the prospect of the plain of Italy from Monte Mottarone. It does not matter whether it is human or inhuman, or whether it leaves you thinking deeply or radiantly but superficially pleased. Some things are more easily done as short stories than others and more abundantly done, but one of the many pleasures of short-story writing is to achieve the impossible.

At any rate, that is the present writer's conception of the art of the short story, as the jolly art of making something very bright and moving; it may be horrible or pathetic or funny or beautiful or profoundly illuminating, having only this essential, that it should take from fifteen to fifty minutes to read aloud. All the rest is just whatever invention and imagination and the mood can give—a vision of buttered slides on a busy day or of unprecedented worlds. In that spirit of miscellaneous expectation these stories should be received. Each is intended to be a thing by itself; and if it is not too ungrateful to kindly and enterprising publishers, I would confess I would much prefer to see each printed expensively alone, and left in a little brown-paper cover to lie about a room against the needs of a quite casual curiosity. And I would rather this volume were found in the bedrooms of convalescents and in dentists' parlours and railway trains than in gentlemen's studies. I would rather have it dipped in and dipped in again than read severely through. Essentially it is a miscellany of inventions, many of which were very pleasant to write; and its end is more than attained if some of them are refreshing and agreeable to read. I have now re-read them all, and I am glad to think I wrote them. I like them, but I cannot tell how much the associations of old happinesses gives them a flavour for me. I make no claims for them and no apology; they will be read as long as people read them. Things written either live or die; unless it be for a place of judgment upon Academic impostors, there is no apologetic intermediate state.

I may add that I have tried to set a date to most of these stories, but that they are not arranged in strictly chronological order.

H. G. WELLS.

CONTENTS.

I.

THE JILTING OF JANE.

As I sit writing in my study, I can hear our Jane bumping her way downstairs with a brush and dust-pan. She used in the old days to sing hymn tunes, or the British national song for the time being, to these instruments, but latterly she has been silent and even careful over her work. Time was when I prayed with fervour for such silence, and my wife with sighs for such care, but now they have come we are not so glad as we might have anticipated we should be. Indeed, I would rejoice secretly, though it may be unmanly weakness to admit it, even to hear Jane sing "Daisy," or, by the fracture of any plate but one of Euphemia's best green ones, to learn that the period of brooding has come to an end.

Yet how we longed to hear the last of Jane's young man before we heard the last of him! Jane was always very free with her conversation to my wife, and discoursed admirably in the kitchen on a variety of topics—so well, indeed, that I sometimes left my study door open—our house is a small one—to partake of it. But after William came, it was always William, nothing but William; William this and William that; and when we thought William was worked out and exhausted altogether, then William all over again. The engagement lasted altogether three years;

yet how she got introduced to William, and so became thus saturated with him, was always a secret. For my part, I believe it was at the street corner where the Rev. Barnabas Baux used to hold an open-air service after evensong on Sundays. Young Cupids were wont to flit like moths round the paraffin flare of that centre of High Church hymn-singing. I fancy she stood singing hymns there, out of memory and her imagination, instead of coming home to get supper, and William came up beside her and said, "Hello!" "Hello yourself!" she said; and etiquette being satisfied, they proceeded to talk together.

As Euphemia has a reprehensible way of letting her servants talk to her, she soon heard of him. "He is such a respectable young man, ma'am," said Jane, "you don't know." Ignoring the slur cast on her acquaintance, my wife inquired further about this William.

"He is second porter at Maynard's, the draper's," said Jane, "and gets eighteen shillings—nearly a pound—a week, m'm; and when the head porter leaves he will be head porter. His relatives are quite superior people, m'm. Not labouring people at all. His father was a greengrosher, m'm, and had a churnor, and he was bankrup' twice. And one of his sisters is in a Home for the Dying. It will be a very good match for me, m'm," said Jane, "me being an orphan girl."

"Then you are engaged to him?" asked my wife.

"Not engaged, ma'am; but he is saving money to buy a ring—hammyfist."

"Well, Jane, when you are properly engaged to him you may ask him round here on Sunday afternoons, and have tea with him in the kitchen;" for my Euphemia has a motherly conception of her duty towards her maid-servants. And presently the amethystine ring was being worn about the house, even with ostentation, and Jane developed a new way of bringing in the joint so that this gage was evident. The elder Miss Maitland was aggrieved by it, and told my wife that servants ought not to wear rings. But my wife looked it up in Enquire Within and Mrs. Motherly's Book of Household Management, and found no prohibition. So Jane remained with this happiness added to her love.

The treasure of Jane's heart appeared to me to be what respectable people call a very deserving young man. "William, ma'am," said Jane one day suddenly, with ill-concealed complacency, as she counted out the beer bottles, "William, ma'am, is a teetotaller. Yes, m'm; and he don't smoke. Smoking, ma'am," said Jane, as one who reads the heart, "do make such a dust about. Beside the waste of money. And the smell. However, I suppose they got to do it—some of them..."

William was at first a rather shabby young man of the ready-made black coat school of costume. He had watery gray eyes, and a complexion appropriate to the brother of one in a Home for the Dying. Euphemia did not fancy him very much, even at the beginning. His eminent respectability was vouched for by an alpaca umbrella, from which he never allowed himself to be parted.

"He goes to chapel," said Jane. "His papa, ma'am——"

"His what, Jane?"

"His papa, ma'am, was Church: but Mr. Maynard is a Plymouth Brother, and William thinks it Policy, ma'am, to go there too. Mr. Maynard comes and talks to him quite friendly when they ain't busy, about using up all the ends of string, and about his soul. He takes a lot of notice, do Mr. Maynard, of William, and the way he saves his soul, ma'am."

Presently we heard that the head porter at Maynard's had left, and that William was head porter at twenty-three shillings a week. "He is really kind of over the man who drives the van," said Jane, "and him married, with three children." And she promised in the pride of her heart to make interest for us with William to favour us so that we might get our parcels of drapery from Maynard's with exceptional promptitude.

After this promotion a rapidly-increasing prosperity came upon Jane's young man. One day we learned that Mr. Maynard had given William a book. "'Smiles' 'Elp Yourself,' it's called," said Jane; "but it ain't comic. It tells you how to get on in the world, and some what William read to me was lovely, ma'am."

Euphemia told me of this, laughing, and then she became suddenly grave. "Do you know, dear," she said, "Jane said one thing I did not like. She had been quiet for a minute, and then she suddenly remarked, 'William is a lot above me, ma'am, ain't he?'"

"I don't see anything in that," I said, though later my eyes were to be opened.

One Sunday afternoon about that time I was sitting at my writing-desk— possibly I was reading a good book—when a something went by the window. I heard a startled exclamation behind me, and saw Euphemia with her hands clasped together and her eyes dilated. "George," she said in an awe-stricken whisper, "did you see?"

Then we both spoke to one another at the same moment, slowly and solemnly: "A silk hat! Yellow gloves! A new umbrella!"

"It may be my fancy, dear," said Euphemia; "but his tie was very like yours. I believe Jane keeps him in ties. She told me a little while ago, in a way that implied volumes about the rest of your costume, 'The master do wear pretty ties, ma'am.' And he echoes all your novelties."

The young couple passed our window again on their way to their customary walk. They were arm in arm. Jane looked exquisitely proud, happy, and uncomfortable, with new white cotton gloves, and William, in the silk hat, singularly genteel!

That was the culmination of Jane's happiness. When she returned, "Mr. Maynard has been talking to William, ma'am," she said, "and he is to serve customers, just like the young shop gentlemen, during the next sale. And if he gets on, he is to be made an assistant, ma'am, at the first opportunity. He has got to be as gentlemanly as he can, ma'am; and if he ain't, ma'am, he says it won't be for want of trying. Mr. Maynard has took a great fancy to him."

"He is getting on, Jane," said my wife.

"Yes, ma'am," said Jane thoughtfully; "he is getting on."

And she sighed.

That next Sunday as I drank my tea I interrogated my wife. "How is this Sunday different from all other Sundays, little woman? What has happened? Have you altered the curtains, or re-arranged the furniture, or where is the indefinable difference of it? Are you wearing your hair in a new way without warning me? I perceive a change clearly, and I cannot for the life of me say what it is."

Then my wife answered in her most tragic voice, "George," she said, "that William has not come near the place to-day! And Jane is crying her heart out upstairs."

There followed a period of silence. Jane, as I have said, stopped singing about the house, and began to care for our brittle possessions, which struck my wife as being a very sad sign indeed. The next Sunday, and the next, Jane asked to go out, "to walk with William," and my wife, who never attempts to extort confidences, gave her permission, and asked no questions. On each occasion Jane came back looking flushed and very determined. At last one day she became communicative.

"William is being led away," she remarked abruptly, with a catching of the breath, apropos of tablecloths. "Yes, m'm. She is a milliner, and she can play on the piano."

"I thought," said my wife, "that you went out with him on Sunday."

"Not out with him, m'm—after him. I walked along by the side of them, and told her he was engaged to me."

"Dear me, Jane, did you? What did they do?"

"Took no more notice of me than if I was dirt. So I told her she should suffer for it."

"It could not have been a very agreeable walk, Jane."

"Not for no parties, ma'am."

"I wish," said Jane, "I could play the piano, ma'am. But anyhow, I don't mean to let her get him away from me. She's older than him, and her hair ain't gold to the roots, ma'am."

It was on the August Bank Holiday that the crisis came. We do not clearly know the details of the fray, but only such fragments as poor Jane let fall. She came home dusty, excited, and with her heart hot within her.

The milliner's mother, the milliner, and William had made a party to the Art Museum at South Kensington, I think. Anyhow, Jane had calmly but firmly accosted them somewhere in the streets, and asserted her right to what, in spite of the consensus of literature, she held to be her inalienable property. She did, I think, go so far as to lay hands on him. They dealt with her in a crushingly superior way. They "called a cab." There was a "scene," William being pulled away into the four-wheeler by his future wife and mother-in-law from the reluctant hands of our discarded Jane. There were threats of giving her "in charge."

"My poor Jane!" said my wife, mincing veal as though she was mincing William. "It's a shame of them. I would think no more of him. He is not worthy of you."

"No, m'm," said Jane. "He is weak.

"But it's that woman has done it," said Jane. She was never known to bring herself to pronounce "that woman's" name or to admit her girlishness. "I can't think what minds some women must have—to try and get a girl's young man away from her. But there, it only hurts to talk about it," said Jane.

Thereafter our house rested from William. But there was something in the manner of Jane's scrubbing the front doorstep or sweeping out the rooms, a certain viciousness, that persuaded me that the story had not yet ended.

"Please, m'm, may I go and see a wedding tomorrow?" said Jane one day.

My wife knew by instinct whose wedding. "Do you think it is wise, Jane?" she said.

"I would like to see the last of him," said Jane.

"My dear," said my wife, fluttering into my room about twenty minutes after Jane had started, "Jane has been to the boot-hole and taken all the left-off boots and shoes, and gone off to the wedding with them in a bag. Surely she cannot mean—"

"Jane," I said, "is developing character. Let us hope for the best."

Jane came back with a pale, hard face. All the boots seemed to be still in her bag, at which my wife heaved a premature sigh of relief. We heard her go upstairs and replace the boots with considerable emphasis.

"Quite a crowd at the wedding, ma'am," she said presently, in a purely conversational style, sitting in our little kitchen, and scrubbing the potatoes; "and such a lovely day for them." She proceeded to numerous other details, clearly avoiding some cardinal incident.

"It was all extremely respectable and nice, ma'am; but her father didn't wear a black coat, and looked quite out of place, ma'am. Mr. Piddingquirk—"

"Who?"

"Mr. Piddingquirk—William that was, ma'am—had white gloves, and a coat like a clergyman, and a lovely chrysanthemum. He looked so nice, ma'am. And there was red carpet down, just like for gentlefolks. And they say he gave the clerk four shillings, ma'am. It was a real kerridge they had—not a fly. When they came out of church there was rice-throwing, and her two little sisters dropping dead flowers. And someone threw a slipper, and then I threw a boot—"

"Threw a boot, Jane!"

"Yes, ma'am. Aimed at her. But it hit him. Yes, ma'am, hard. Gev him a black eye, I should think. I only threw that one. I hadn't the heart to try again. All the little boys cheered when it hit him."

After an interval—"I am sorry the boot hit him."

Another pause. The potatoes were being scrubbed violently. "He always was a bit above me, you know, ma'am. And he was led away."

The potatoes were more than finished. Jane rose sharply with a sigh, and rapped the basin down on the table.

"I don't care," she said. "I don't care a rap. He will find out his mistake yet. It serves me right. I was stuck up about him. I ought not to have looked so high. And I am glad things are as things are."

My wife was in the kitchen, seeing to the higher cookery. After the confession of the boot-throwing, she must have watched poor Jane fuming with a certain dismay in those brown eyes of hers. But I imagine they softened again very quickly, and then Jane's must have met them.

"Oh, ma'am," said Jane, with an astonishing change of note, "think of all that might have been! Oh, ma'am, I could have been so happy! I ought to have known, but I didn't know...You're very kind to let me talk to you, ma'am...for it's hard on me, ma'am...it's har-r-r-r-d—"

And I gather that Euphemia so far forgot herself as to let Jane sob out some of the fullness of her heart on a sympathetic shoulder. My Euphemia, thank Heaven, has never properly grasped the importance of "keeping up her position." And since that fit of weeping, much of the accent of bitterness has gone out of Jane's scrubbing and brush work.

Indeed, something passed the other day with the butcher-boy—but that scarcely belongs to this story. However, Jane is young still, and time and change are at work with her. We all have our sorrows, but I do not believe very much in the existence of sorrows that never heal.

II.

THE CONE.

The night was hot and overcast, the sky red-rimmed with the lingering sunset of midsummer. They sat at the open window, trying to fancy the air was fresher there. The trees and shrubs of the garden stood stiff and dark; beyond in the roadway a gas-lamp burnt, bright orange against the hazy blue of the evening. Farther were the three lights of the railway signal against the lowering sky. The man and woman spoke to one another in low tones.

"He does not suspect?" said the man, a little nervously.

"Not he," she said peevishly, as though that too irritated her. "He thinks of nothing but the works and the prices of fuel. He has no imagination, no poetry."

"None of these men of iron have," he said sententiously. "They have no hearts."

"He has not," she said. She turned her discontented face towards the window. The distant sound of a roaring and rushing drew nearer and grew in volume; the house quivered; one heard the metallic rattle of the tender. As the train passed, there was a glare of light above the cutting and a driving tumult of smoke; one, two, three, four, five, six, seven, eight black oblongs—eight trucks—passed across the dim grey of the embankment, and were suddenly extinguished one by one in the throat of the tunnel, which, with the last, seemed to swallow down train, smoke, and sound in one abrupt gulp.

"This country was all fresh and beautiful once," he said; "and now—it is Gehenna. Down that way—nothing but pot-banks and chimneys belching fire and dust into the face of heaven...But what does it matter? An end comes, an end to all this cruelty...To-morrow." He spoke the last word in a whisper.

"To-morrow," she said, speaking in a whisper too, and still staring out of the window.

"Dear!" he said, putting his hand on hers.

She turned with a start, and their eyes searched one another's. Hers softened to his gaze. "My dear one!" she said, and then: "It seems so strange—that you should have come into my life like this—to open—" She paused.

"To open?" he said.

"All this wonderful world"—she hesitated, and spoke still more softly— "this world of love to me."

Then suddenly the door clicked and closed. They turned their heads, and he started violently back. In the shadow of the room stood a great shadowy figure-silent. They saw the face dimly in the half-light, with unexpressive dark patches under the pent-house brows. Every muscle in Raut's body suddenly became tense. When could the door have opened? What had he heard? Had he heard all? What had he seen? A tumult of questions.

The new-comer's voice came at last, after a pause that seemed interminable. "Well?" he said.

"I was afraid I had missed you, Horrocks," said the man at the window, gripping the window-ledge with his hand. His voice was unsteady.

The clumsy figure of Horrocks came forward out of the shadow. He made no answer to Raut's remark. For a moment he stood above them.

The woman's heart was cold within her. "I told Mr. Raut it was just possible you might come back," she said in a voice that never quivered.

Horrocks, still silent, sat down abruptly in the chair by her little work-table. His big hands were clenched; one saw now the fire of his eyes under the shadow of his brows. He was trying to get his breath. His eyes went from the woman he had trusted to the friend he had trusted, and then back to the woman.

By this time and for the moment all three half understood one another.

Yet none dared say a word to ease the pent-up things that choked them.

It was the husband's voice that broke the silence at last.

"You wanted to see me?" he said to Raut.

Raut started as he spoke. "I came to see you," he said, resolved to lie to the last.

"Yes," said Horrocks.

"You promised," said Raut, "to show me some fine effects of moonlight and smoke."

"I promised to show you some fine effects of moonlight and smoke," repeated Horrocks in a colourless voice.

"And I thought I might catch you to-night before you went down to the works," proceeded Raut, "and come with you."

There was another pause. Did the man mean to take the thing coolly? Did he, after all, know? How long had he been in the room? Yet even at the moment when they heard the door, their attitudes ... Horrocks glanced at the profile of the woman, shadowy pallid in the half-light. Then he glanced at Raut, and seemed to recover himself suddenly. "Of course," he said, "I promised to show you the works under their proper dramatic conditions. It's odd how I could have forgotten."

"If I am troubling you—" began Raut.

Horrocks started again. A new light had suddenly come into the sultry gloom of his eyes. "Not in the least." he said.

"Have you been telling Mr. Raut of all these contrasts of flame and shadow you think so splendid?" said the woman, turning now to her husband for the first time, her confidence creeping back again, her voice just one half-note too high—"that dreadful theory of yours that machinery is beautiful, and everything else in the world ugly. I thought he would not spare you, Mr. Raut. It's his great theory, his one discovery in art."

"I am slow to make discoveries," said Horrocks grimly, damping her suddenly. "But what I discover ..." He stopped.

"Well?" she said.

"Nothing;" and suddenly he rose to his feet.

"I promised to show you the works," he said to Raut, and put his big, clumsy hand on his friend's shoulder. "And you are ready to go?"

"Quite," said Raut, and stood up also.

There was another pause. Each of them peered through the indistinctness of the dusk at the other two.

Horrocks' hand still rested on Raut's shoulder. Raut half fancied still that the incident was trivial after all. But Mrs. Horrocks knew her husband better, knew that grim quiet in his voice, and the confusion in her mind took a vague shape of physical evil. "Very well," said Horrocks, and, dropping his hand, turned towards the door.

"My hat?" Raut looked round in the half-light.

"That's my work-basket," said Mrs. Horrocks with a gust of hysterical laughter. Their hands came together on the back of the chair. "Here it is!" he said. She had an impulse to warn him in an undertone, but she could not frame a word. "Don't go!"

and "Beware of him!" struggled in her mind, and the swift moment passed.

"Got it?" said Horrocks, standing with the door half open.

Raut stepped towards him. "Better say goodbye to Mrs. Horrocks," said the ironmaster, even more grimly quiet in his tone than before.

Raut started and turned. "Good-evening, Mrs. Horrocks," he said, and their hands touched.

Horrocks held the door open with a ceremonial politeness unusual in him towards men. Raut went out, and then, after a wordless look at her, her husband followed. She stood motionless while Raut's light footfall and her husband's heavy tread, like bass and treble, passed down the passage together. The front door slammed heavily. She went to the window, moving slowly, and stood watching, leaning forward. The two men appeared for a moment at the gateway in the road, passed under the street lamp, and were hidden by the black masses of the shrubbery. The lamplight fell for a moment on their faces, showing only unmeaning pale patches, telling nothing of what she still feared, and doubted, and craved vainly to know. Then she sank down into a crouching attitude in the big arm-chair, her eyes-wide open and staring out at the red lights from the furnaces that flickered in the sky. An hour after she was still there, her attitude scarcely changed.

The oppressive stillness of the evening weighed heavily upon Raut. They went side by side down the road in silence, and in silence turned into the cinder-made byway that presently opened out the prospect of the valley.

A blue haze, half dust, half mist, touched the long valley with mystery. Beyond were Hanley and Etruria, grey and dark masses, outlined thinly by the rare golden dots of the street lamps, and here and there a gas-lit window, or the yellow glare of some late-working factory or crowded public-house. Out of the masses, clear and slender against the evening sky, rose a multitude of tall chimneys, many of them reeking, a few smokeless during a season of "play." Here and there a pallid patch and ghostly stunted beehive shapes showed the position of a pot-bank or a wheel, black and sharp against the hot lower sky, marked some colliery where they raise the iridescent coal of the place. Nearer at hand was the broad stretch of railway, and half-invisible trains shunted—a steady puffing and rumbling, with every run a ringing concussion and a rhymthic series of impacts, and a passage of intermittent puffs of white steam across the further view. And to the left, between the railway and the dark mass of the low hill beyond, dominating the whole view, colossal, inky-black, and crowned with smoke and fitful flames, stood the great cylinders of the Jeddah Company Blast Furnaces, the central edifices of the big ironworks of which Horrocks was the manager. They stood heavy and threatening, full of an incessant turmoil of flames and seething molten iron, and about the feet of them rattled the rolling-mills, and the steam-hammer beat heavily and splashed the white iron sparks hither and thither. Even as they looked, a truckful of fuel was shot into one of the giants, and the red flames gleamed out, and a confusion of smoke and black dust came boiling upwards towards the sky.

"Certainly you get some colour with your furnaces," said Raut, breaking a silence that had become apprehensive.

Horrocks grunted. He stood with his hands in his pockets, frowning down at the dim steaming railway and the busy ironworks beyond, frowning as if he were thinking out some knotty problem.

Raut glanced at him and away again. "At present your moonlight effect is hardly ripe," he continued, looking upward; "the moon is still smothered by the vestiges of daylight."

Horrocks stared at him with the expression of a man who has suddenly awakened. "Vestiges of daylight? ... Of course, of course." He too looked up at the moon, pale still in the midsummer sky. "Come along," he said suddenly, and gripping Raut's arm in his hand, made a move towards the path that dropped from them to the railway.

Raut hung back. Their eyes met and saw a thousand things in a moment that their lips came near to say. Horrocks's hand tightened and then relaxed. He let go, and before Raut was aware of it, they were arm in arm, and walking, one unwillingly enough, down the path.

"You see the fine effect of the railway signals towards Burslem," said Horrocks, suddenly breaking into loquacity, striding fast and tightening the grip of his elbow the while—"little green lights and red and white lights, all against the haze. You have an eye for effect, Raut. It's fine. And look at those furnaces of mine, how they rise upon us as we come down the hill. That to the right is my pet—seventy feet of him. I packed him myself, and he's boiled away cheerfully with iron in his guts for five long years. I've a particular fancy for him. That line of red there—a lovely bit of warm orange you'd call it, Raut—that's the puddlers' furnaces, and there, in the hot light, three black figures—did you see the white splash of the steam-hammer then?—that's the rolling mills. Come along! Clang, clatter, how it goes rattling across the floor! Sheet tin, Raut,—amazing stuff. Glass mirrors are not in it when that stuff comes from the mill. And, squelch! there goes the hammer again. Come along!"

He had to stop talking to catch at his breath. His arm twisted into Raut's with benumbing tightness. He had come striding down the black path towards the railway as though he was possessed. Raut had not spoken a word, had simply hung back against Horrocks's pull with all his strength.

"I say," he said now, laughing nervously, but with an undertone of snarl in his voice, "why on earth are you nipping my arm off, Horrocks, and dragging me along like this?"

At length Horrocks released him. His manner changed again. "Nipping your arm off?" he said. "Sorry. But it's you taught me the trick of walking in that friendly way."

"You haven't learnt the refinements of it yet then," said Raut, laughing artificially again. "By Jove! I'm black and blue." Horrocks offered no apology. They stood now near the bottom of the hill, close to the fence that bordered the railway. The ironworks had grown larger and spread out with their approach. They looked up to the blast furnaces now instead of down; the further view of Etruria and Hanley had dropped out of sight with their descent. Before them, by the stile, rose a notice-board, bearing, still dimly visible, the words, "BEWARE OF THE TRAINS," half hidden by splashes of coaly mud.

"Fine effects," said Horrocks, waving his arm. "Here comes a train. The puffs of smoke, the orange glare, the round eye of light in front of it, the melodious rattle. Fine effects! But these furnaces of mine used to be finer, before we shoved cones in their throats, and saved the gas."

"How?" said Raut. "Cones?"

"Cones, my man, cones. I'll show you one nearer. The flames used to flare out of the open throats, great—what is it?—pillars of cloud by day, red and black smoke, and pillars of fire by night. Now we run it off—in pipes, and burn it to heat the blast, and the top is shut by a cone. You'll be interested in that cone."

"But every now and then," said Raut, "you get a burst of fire and smoke up there."

"The cone's not fixed, it's hung by a chain from a lever, and balanced by an equipoise. You shall see it nearer. Else, of course, there'd be no way of getting fuel into the thing. Every now and then the cone dips, and out comes the flare."

"I see," said Raut. He looked over his shoulder. "The moon gets brighter," he said.

"Come along," said Horrocks abruptly, gripping his shoulder again, and moving him suddenly towards the railway crossing. And then came one of those swift incidents, vivid, but so rapid that they leave one doubtful and reeling. Half-way across, Horrocks's hand suddenly clenched upon him like a vice, and swung him backward and through a half-turn, so that he looked up the line. And there a chain of lamp-lit carriage windows telescoped swiftly as it came towards them, and the red and yellow lights of an engine grew larger and larger, rushing down upon them. As he grasped what this meant, he turned his face to Horrocks, and pushed with all his strength against the arm that held him back between the rails. The struggle did not last a moment. Just as certain as it was that Horrocks held him there, so certain was it that he had been violently lugged out of danger.

"Out of the way," said Horrocks with a gasp, as the train came rattling by, and they stood panting by the gate into the ironworks.

"I did not see it coming," said Raut, still, even in spite of his own apprehensions, trying to keep up an appearance of ordinary intercourse.

Horrocks answered with a grunt. "The cone," he said, and then, as one who recovers himself, "I thought you did not hear."

"I didn't," said Raut.

"I wouldn't have had you run over then for the world," said Horrocks.

"For a moment I lost my nerve," said Raut.

Horrocks stood for half a minute, then turned abruptly towards the ironworks again. "See how fine these great mounds of mine, these clinker-heaps, look in the night! That truck yonder, up above there! Up it goes, and out-tilts the slag. See the palpitating red stuff go sliding down the slope. As we get nearer, the heap rises up and cuts the blast furnaces. See the quiver up above the big one. Not that way! This way, between the heaps. That goes to the puddling furnaces, but I want to show you the canal first." He came and took Raut by the elbow, and so they went along side by side. Raut answered Horrocks vaguely. What, he asked himself, had really happened on the line? Was he deluding himself with his own fancies, or had Horrocks actually held him back in the way of the train? Had he just been within an ace of being murdered?

Suppose this slouching, scowling monster did know anything? For a minute or two then Raut was really afraid for his life, but the mood passed as he reasoned with himself. After all, Horrocks might have heard nothing. At any rate, he had pulled him out of the way in time. His odd manner might be due to the mere vague jealousy he had shown once before. He was talking now of the ash-heaps and the canal. "Eigh?" said Horrocks.

"What?" said Raut. "Rather! The haze in the moonlight. Fine!"

"Our canal," said Horrocks, stopping suddenly. "Our canal by moonlight and firelight is immense. You've never seen it? Fancy that! You've spent too many of your evenings philandering up in Newcastle there. I tell you, for real florid quality——But you shall see. Boiling water ..."

As they came out of the labyrinth of clinker-heaps and mounds of coal and ore, the noises of the rolling-mill sprang upon them suddenly, loud, near, and distinct. Three shadowy workmen went by and touched their caps to Horrocks. Their faces were vague in the darkness. Raut felt a futile impulse to address them, and before he could frame his words they passed into the shadows. Horrocks pointed to the canal close before them now: a weird-looking place it seemed, in the blood-red reflections of the furnaces. The hot water that cooled the tuyères came into it, some fifty yards up—a tumultuous, almost boiling affluent, and the steam rose up from the water in silent white wisps and streaks, wrapping damply about them, an incessant succession of ghosts coming up from the black and red eddies, a white uprising that made the head swim. The shining black tower of the larger blast-furnace rose overhead out of the mist, and its tumultuous riot filled their ears. Raut kept away from the edge of the water, and watched Horrocks.

"Here it is red," said Horrocks, "blood-red vapour as red and hot as sin; but yonder there, where the moonlight falls on it, and it drives across the clinker-heaps, it is as white as death."

Raut turned his head for a moment, and then came back hastily to his watch on Horrocks. "Come along to the rolling-mills," said Horrocks. The threatening hold was not so evident that time, and Raut felt a little reassured. But all the same, what on earth did Horrocks mean about "white as death" and "red as sin"? Coincidence, perhaps?

They went and stood behind the puddlers for a little while, and then through the rolling-mills, where amidst an incessant din the deliberate steam-hammer beat the juice out of the succulent iron, and black, half-naked Titans rushed the plastic bars, like hot sealing-wax, between the wheels, "Come on," said Horrocks in Raut's ear; and they went and peeped through the little glass hole behind the tuyères, and saw the tumbled fire writhing in the pit of the blast-furnace. It left one eye blinded for a while. Then, with green and blue patches dancing across the dark, they went to the lift by which the trucks of ore and fuel and lime were raised to the top of the big cylinder.

And out upon the narrow rail that overhung the furnace Raut's doubts came upon him again. Was it wise to be here? If Horrocks did know—everything! Do what he would, he could not resist a violent trembling. Right under foot was a sheer depth of seventy feet. It was a dangerous place. They pushed by a truck of fuel to get to the railing that crowned the thing. The reek of the furnace, a sulphurous vapour streaked with pungent bitterness, seemed to make the distant hillside of Hanley quiver. The moon was riding out now from among a drift of clouds, half-way up the sky above the undulating wooded outlines of Newcastle. The steaming canal ran away from below them under an indistinct bridge, and vanished into the dim haze of the flat fields towards Burslem.

"That's the cone I've been telling you of," shouted Horrocks; "and, below that, sixty feet of fire and molten metal, with the air of the blast frothing through it like gas in soda-water."

Raut gripped the hand-rail tightly, and stared down at the cone. The heat was intense. The boiling of the iron and the tumult of the blast made a thunderous accompaniment to Horrocks's voice. But the thing had to be gone through now. Perhaps, after all...

"In the middle," bawled Horrocks, "temperature near a thousand degrees. If you were dropped into it ... flash into flame like a pinch of gunpowder in a candle. Put your hand out and feel the heat of his breath. Why, even up here I've seen the rain-water boiling off the trucks. And that cone there. It's a damned sight too hot for roasting cakes. The top side of it's three hundred degrees."

"Three hundred degrees!" said Raut.

"Three hundred centigrade, mind!" said Horrocks. "It will boil the blood out of you in no time."

"Eigh?" said Raut, and turned.

"Boil the blood out of you in ... No, you don't!"

"Let me go!" screamed Raut. "Let go my arm!"

With one hand he clutched at the hand-rail, then with both. For a moment the two men stood swaying. Then suddenly, with a violent jerk, Horrocks had twisted him from his hold. He clutched at Horrocks and missed, his foot went back into empty air; in mid-air he twisted himself, and then cheek and shoulder and knee struck the hot cone together.

He clutched the chain by which the cone hung, and the thing sank an infinitesimal amount as he struck it. A circle of glowing red appeared about him, and a tongue of flame, released from the chaos within, flickered up towards him. An intense pain assailed him at the knees, and he could smell the singeing of his hands. He raised himself to his feet, and tried to climb up the chain, and then something struck his head. Black and shining with the moonlight, the throat of the furnace rose about him.

Horrocks, he saw, stood above him by one of the trucks of fuel on the rail. The gesticulating figure was bright and white in the moonlight, and shouting, "Fizzle, you fool! Fizzle, you hunter of women! You hot-blooded hound! Boil! boil! boil!"

Suddenly he caught up a handful of coal out of the truck, and flung it deliberately, lump after lump, at Raut.

"Horrocks!" cried Raut. "Horrocks!"

He clung, crying, to the chain, pulling himself up from the burning of the cone. Each missile Horrocks flung hit him. His clothes charred and glowed, and as he struggled the cone dropped, and a rush of hot, suffocating gas whooped out and burned round him in a swift breath of flame.

His human likeness departed from him. When the momentary red had passed, Horrocks saw a charred, blackened figure, its head streaked with blood, still clutching and fumbling with the chain, and writhing in agony—a cindery animal, an inhuman, monstrous creature that began a sobbing, intermittent shriek.

Abruptly at the sight the ironmaster's anger passed. A deadly sickness came upon him. The heavy odour of burning flesh came drifting up to his nostrils. His sanity returned to him.

"God have mercy upon me!" he cried. "O God! what have I done?"

He knew the thing below him, save that it still moved and felt, was already a dead man—that the blood of the poor wretch must be boiling in his veins. An intense realisation of that agony came to his mind, and overcame every other feeling. For a moment he stood irresolute, and then, turning to the truck, he hastily tilted its contents upon the struggling thing that had once been a man. The mass fell with a thud, and went radiating over the cone. With the thud the shriek ended, and a boiling confusion of smoke, dust, and flame came rushing up towards him. As it passed, he saw the cone clear again.

Then he staggered back, and stood trembling, clinging to the rail with both hands. His lips moved, but no words came to them.

Down below was the sound of voices and running steps. The clangour of rolling in the shed ceased abruptly.

III.

THE STOLEN BACILLUS.

"This again," said the Bacteriologist, slipping a glass slide under the microscope, "is well,—a preparation of the Bacillus of cholera—the cholera germ."

The pale-faced man peered down the microscope. He was evidently not accustomed to that kind of thing, and held a limp white hand over his disengaged eye. "I see very little," he said.

"Touch this screw," said the Bacteriologist; "perhaps the microscope is out of focus for you. Eyes vary so much. Just the fraction of a turn this way or that."

"Ah! now I see," said the visitor. "Not so very much to see after all. Little streaks and shreds of pink. And yet those little particles, those mere atomies, might multiply and devastate a city! Wonderful!"

He stood up, and releasing the glass slip from the microscope, held it in his hand towards the window. "Scarcely visible," he said, scrutinising the preparation. He hesitated. "Are these—alive? Are they dangerous now?"

"Those have been stained and killed," said the Bacteriologist. "I wish, for my own part, we could kill and stain every one of them in the universe."

"I suppose," the pale man said, with a slight smile, 'that you scarcely care to have such things about you in the living—in the active state?"

"On the contrary, we are obliged to," said the Bacteriologist. "Here, for instance—" He walked across the room and took up one of several sealed tubes. "Here is the living thing. This is a cultivation of the actual living disease bacteria." He hesitated. "Bottled cholera, so to speak."

A slight gleam of satisfaction appeared momentarily in the face of the pale man. "It's a deadly thing to have in your possession," he said, devouring the little tube with his eyes. The Bacteriologist watched the morbid pleasure in his visitor's expression. This man, who had visited him that afternoon with a note of introduction from an old friend, interested him from the very contrast of their dispositions. The lank black hair and deep grey eyes, the haggard expression and nervous manner, the fitful yet keen interest of his visitor were a novel change from the phlegmatic deliberations of the ordinary scientific worker with whom the Bacteriologist chiefly associated. It was perhaps natural, with a hearer evidently so impressionable to the lethal nature of; his topic, to take the most effective aspect of the matter.

He held the tube in his hand thoughtfully. "Yes, here is the pestilence imprisoned. Only break such a little tube as this into a supply of drinking-water, say to these minute particles of life that one must needs stain and examine with the highest powers of the microscope even to see, and that one can neither smell nor taste—say to them, 'Go forth, increase and multiply, and replenish the cisterns,' and death—mysterious, untraceable death, death swift and terrible, death full of pain and indignity—would be released upon this city, and go hither and thither seeking his victims. Here he would take the husband from the wife, here the child from its mother, here the statesman from his duty, and here the toiler from his trouble. He would follow the water-mains, creeping along streets, picking out and punishing a house here and a house there where they did not boil their drinking-water, creeping into the wells of the mineral water makers, getting washed into salad, and lying dormant in ices. He would wait ready to be drunk in the horse-troughs, and by unwary children in the public fountains. He would soak into the soil, to reappear in springs and wells at a thousand unexpected places. Once start him at the water supply, and before we could ring him in, and catch him again, he would have decimated the metropolis."

He stopped abruptly. He had been told rhetoric was his weakness.

"But he is quite safe here, you know—quite safe."

The pale-faced man nodded. His eyes shone. He cleared his throat. "These Anarchist—rascals," said he, "are fools, blind fools—to use bombs when this kind of thing is attainable. I think——"

A gentle rap, a mere light touch of the finger-nails, was heard at the door. The Bacteriologist opened if. "Just a minute, dear," whispered his wife.

When he re-entered the laboratory his visitor was looking at his watch. "I had no idea I had wasted an hour of your time," he said. "Twelve minutes to four. I ought to have left here by half-past three. But your things were really too interesting. No, positively I cannot stop a moment longer. I have an engagement at four."

He passed out of the room reiterating his thanks, and the Bacteriologist accompanied him to the door, and then returned thoughtfully along the passage to his laboratory. He was musing on the ethnology of his visitor. Certainly the man was not a Teutonic type nor a common Latin one. "A morbid product, anyhow, I am afraid," said the Bacteriologist to himself. "How he gloated over those cultivations of disease germs!" A disturbing thought struck him. He turned to the bench by the vapour bath, and then very quickly to his writing-table. Then he felt hastily in his pockets and then rushed to the door. "I may have put it down on the hall table," he said.

"Minnie!" he shouted hoarsely in the hall.

"Yes, dear," came a remote voice.

"Had I anything in my hand when I spoke to you, dear, just now?"

Pause.

"Nothing, dear, because I remember——"

"Blue ruin!" cried the Bacteriologist, and incontinently ran to the front door and down the steps of his house to the street.

Minnie, hearing the door slam violently, ran in alarm to the window. Down the street a slender man was getting into a cab. The Bacteriologist, hatless, and in his carpet slippers, was running and gesticulating wildly towards this group. One slipper came off, but he did not wait for it. "He has gone mad!" said Minnie; "it's that horrid science of his"; and, opening the window, would have called after him. The slender man, suddenly glancing round, seemed struck with the same idea of mental disorder. He pointed hastily to the Bacteriologist, said something to the cabman, the apron of the cab slammed, the whip swished, the horse's feet clattered, and in a moment cab and Bacteriologist hotly in pursuit, had receded up the vista of the roadway and disappeared round the corner.

Minnie remained straining out of the window for a minute. Then she drew her head back into the room again. She was dumbfounded. "Of course he is eccentric," she meditated. "But running about London—in the height of the season, too—in his socks!" A happy thought struck her. She hastily put her bonnet on, seized his shoes, went into the hall, took down his hat and light overcoat from the pegs, emerged upon the doorstep, and hailed a cab that opportunely crawled by. "Drive me up the road and round Havelock Crescent, and see if we can find a gentleman running about in a velveteen coat and no hat."

"Velveteen coat, ma'am, and no 'at. Very good, ma'am." And the cabman whipped up at once in the most matter-of-fact way, as if he drove to this address every day in his life.

Some few minutes later the little group of cabmen and loafers that collects round the cabman's shelter at Haverstock Hill were startled by the passing of a cab with a ginger-coloured screw of a horse, driven furiously.

They were silent as it went by, and then as it receded—"That's 'Arry

'Icks. Wot's he got?" said the stout gentleman known as Old

Tootles.

"He's a-using his whip, he is, to rights," said the ostler boy.

"Hullo!" said poor old Tommy Byles; "here's another bloomin' loonatic.

Blowed if there ain't."

"It's old George," said Old Tootles, "and he's drivin' a loonatic, as you say. Ain't he a-clawin' out of the keb? Wonder if he's after 'Arry 'Icks?"

The group round the cabman's shelter became animated. Chorus: "Go it,

George!" "It's a race." "You'll ketch 'em!" "Whip up!"

"She's a goer, she is!" said the ostler boy.

"Strike me giddy!" cried Old Tootles. "Here! I'm a-goin' to begin in a minute. Here's another comin'. If all the cabs in Hampstead ain't gone mad this morning!"

"It's a fieldmale this time," said the ostler boy.

"She's a-followin' him," said Old Tootles. "Usually the other way about."

"What's she got in her 'and?"

"Looks like a 'igh 'at."

"What a bloomin' lark it is! Three to one on old George," said the ostler boy. "Nexst!"

Minnie went by in a perfect roar of applause. She did not like it, but she felt that she was doing her duty, and whirled on down Haverstock Hill and Camden Town High Street with her eyes ever intent on the animated back view of old George, who was driving her vagrant husband so incomprehensibly away from her.

The man in the foremost cab sat crouched in the corner, his arms tightly folded, and the little tube that contained such vast possibilities of destruction gripped in his hand. His mood was a singular mixture of fear and exultation. Chiefly he was afraid of being caught before he could accomplish his purpose, but behind this was a vaguer but larger fear of the awfulness of his crime. But his exultation far exceeded his fear. No Anarchist before him had ever approached this conception of his. Ravachol, Vaillant, all those distinguished persons whose fame he had envied dwindled into insignificance beside him. He had only to make sure of the water supply, and break the little tube into a reservoir. How brilliantly he had planned it, forged the letter of introduction and got into the laboratory, and how brilliantly he had seized his opportunity! The world should hear of him at last. All those people who had sneered at him, neglected him, preferred other people to him, found his company undesirable, should consider him at last. Death, death, death! They had always treated him as a man of no importance. All the world had been in a conspiracy to keep him under. He would teach them yet what it is to isolate a man. What was this familiar street? Great Saint Andrew's Street, of course! How fared the chase? He craned out of the cab. The Bacteriologist was scarcely fifty yards behind. That was bad. He would be caught and stopped yet. He felt in his pocket for money, and found half a sovereign. This he thrust up through the trap in the top of the cab into the man's face. "More," he shouted, "if only we get away."

The money was snatched out of his hand. "Right you are," said the cabman, and the trap slammed, and the lash lay along the glistening side of the horse. The cab swayed, and the Anarchist, half-standing under the trap, put the hand containing the little glass tube upon the apron to preserve his balance. He felt the brittle thing crack, and the broken half of it rang upon the floor of the cab. He fell back into the seat with a curse, and stared dismally at the two or three drops of moisture on the apron.

He shuddered.

"Well, I suppose I shall be the first. Phew! Anyhow, I shall be a Martyr. That's something. But it is a filthy death, nevertheless. I wonder if it hurts as much as they say."

Presently a thought occurred to him—he groped between his feet. A little drop was still in the broken end of the tube, and he drank that to make sure. It was better to make sure. At any rate, he would not fail.

Then it dawned upon him that there was no further need to escape the Bacteriologist. In Wellington Street he told the cabman to stop, and got out. He slipped on the step, and his head felt queer. It was rapid stuff, this cholera poison. He waved his cabman out of existence, so to speak, and stood on the pavement with his arms folded upon his breast awaiting the arrival of the Bacteriologist. There was something tragic in his pose. The sense of imminent death gave him a certain dignity. He greeted his pursuer with a defiant laugh.

"Vive l'Anarchie! You are too late, my friend, I have drunk it. The cholera is abroad!"

The Bacteriologist from his cab beamed curiously at him through his spectacles. "You have drunk it! An Anarchist! I see now." He was about to say something more, and then checked himself. A smile hung in the corner of his mouth. He opened the apron of his cab as if to descend, at which the Anarchist waved him a dramatic farewell and strode off towards Waterloo Bridge, carefully jostling his infected body against as many people as possible. The Bacteriologist was so preoccupied with the vision of him that he scarcely manifested the slightest surprise at the appearance of Minnie upon the pavement with his hat and shoes and overcoat. "Very good of you to bring my things," he said, and remained lost in contemplation of the receding figure of the Anarchist.

"You had better get in," he said, still staring. Minnie felt absolutely convinced now that he was mad, and directed the cabman home on her own responsibility. "Put on my shoes? Certainly, dear," said he, as the cab began to turn, and hid the strutting black figure, now small in the distance, from his eyes. Then suddenly something grotesque struck him, and he laughed. Then he remarked, "It is really very serious, though.

"You see, that man came to my house to see me, and he is an Anarchist. No—don't faint, or I cannot possibly tell you the rest. And I wanted to astonish him, not knowing he was an Anarchist, and took up a cultivation of that new species of Bacterium I was telling you of that infest, and I think cause, the blue patches upon various monkeys; and, like a fool, I said it was Asiatic cholera. And he ran away with it to poison the water of London, and he certainly might have made things look blue for this civilised city. And now he has swallowed it. Of course, I cannot say what will happen, but you know it turned that kitten blue, and the three puppies—in patches, and the sparrow—bright blue. But the bother is, I shall have all the trouble and expense of preparing some more.

"Put on my coat on this hot day! Why? Because we might meet Mrs. Jabber. My dear, Mrs. Jabber is not a draught. But why should I wear a coat on a hot day because of Mrs.——-. Oh! very well."

IV.

THE FLOWERING OF THE STRANGE ORCHID.

The buying of orchids always has in it a certain speculative flavour. You have before you the brown shrivelled lump of tissue, and for the rest you must trust your judgment, or the auctioneer, or your good luck, as your taste may incline. The plant may be moribund or dead, or it may be just a respectable purchase, fair value for your money, or perhaps—for the thing has happened again and again—there slowly unfolds before the delighted eyes of the happy purchaser, day after day, some new variety, some novel richness, a strange twist of the labellum, or some subtler colouration or unexpected mimicry. Pride, beauty, and profit blossom together on one delicate green spike, and, it may be, even immortality. For the new miracle of nature may stand in need of a new specific name, and what so convenient as that of its discoverer? "John-smithia"! There have been worse names.

It was perhaps the hope of some such happy discovery that made Winter Wedderburn such a frequent attendant at these sales—that hope, and also, maybe, the fact that he had nothing else of the slightest interest to do in the world. He was a shy, lonely, rather ineffectual man, provided with just enough income to keep off the spur of necessity, and not enough nervous energy to make him seek any exacting employments. He might have collected stamps or coins, or translated Horace, or bound books, or invented new species of diatoms. But, as it happened, he grew orchids, and had one ambitious little hothouse.

"I have a fancy," he said over his coffee, "that something is going to happen to me to-day." He spoke—as he moved and thought—slowly.

"Oh, don't say that!" said his housekeeper—who was also his remote cousin. For "something happening" was a euphemism that meant only one thing to her.

"You misunderstand me. I mean nothing unpleasant...though what I do mean I scarcely know.

"To-day," he continued, after a pause, "Peters' are going to sell a batch of plants from the Andamans and the Indies. I shall go up and see what they have. It may be I shall buy something good unawares. That may be it."

He passed his cup for his second cupful of coffee.

"Are these the things collected by that poor young fellow you told me of the other day?" asked his cousin, as she filled his cup.

"Yes," he said, and became meditative over a piece of toast.

"Nothing ever does happen to me," he remarked presently, beginning to think aloud. "I wonder why? Things enough happen to other people. There is Harvey. Only the other week; on Monday he picked up sixpence, on Wednesday his chicks all had the staggers, on Friday his cousin came home from Australia, and on Saturday he broke his ankle. What a whirl of excitement!—compared to me."

"I think I would rather be without so much excitement," said his housekeeper. "It can't be good for you."

"I suppose it's troublesome. Still ... you see, nothing ever happens to me. When I was a little boy I never had accidents. I never fell in love as I grew up. Never married... I wonder how it feels to have something happen to you, something really remarkable.

"That orchid-collector was only thirty-six—twenty years younger than myself—when he died. And he had been married twice and divorced once; he had had malarial fever four times, and once he broke his thigh. He killed a Malay once, and once he was wounded by a poisoned dart. And in the end he was killed by jungle-leeches. It must have all been very troublesome, but then it must have been very interesting, you know—except, perhaps, the leeches."

"I am sure it was not good for him," said the lady with conviction.

"Perhaps not." And then Wedderburn looked at his watch. "Twenty-three minutes past eight. I am going up by the quarter to twelve train, so that there is plenty of time. I think I shall wear my alpaca jacket—it is quite warm enough—and my grey felt hat and brown shoes. I suppose—"

He glanced out of the window at the serene sky and sunlit garden, and then nervously at his cousin's face.

"I think you had better take an umbrella if you are going to London," she said in a voice that admitted of no denial. "There's all between here and the station coming back."

When he returned he was in a state of mild excitement. He had made a purchase. It was rare that he could make up his mind quickly enough to buy, but this time he had done so.

"There are Vandas," he said, "and a Dendrobe and some Palaeonophis." He surveyed his purchases lovingly as he consumed his soup. They were laid out on the spotless tablecloth before him, and he was telling his cousin all about them as he slowly meandered through his dinner. It was his custom to live all his visits to London over again in the evening for her and his own entertainment.

"I knew something would happen to-day. And I have bought all these. Some of them—some of them—I feel sure, do you know, that some of them will be remarkable. I don't know how it is, but I feel just as sure as if some one had told me that some of these will turn out remarkable.

"That one "—he pointed to a shrivelled rhizome—"was not identified. It may be a Palaeonophis—or it may not. It may be a new species, or even a new genus. And it was the last that poor Batten ever collected."

"I don't like the look of it," said his housekeeper. "It's such an ugly shape."

"To me it scarcely seems to have a shape."

"I don't like those things that stick out," said his housekeeper.

"It shall be put away in a pot to-morrow."

"It looks," said the housekeeper, "like a spider shamming dead."

Wedderburn smiled and surveyed the root with his head on one side. "It is certainly not a pretty lump of stuff. But you can never judge of these things from their dry appearance. It may turn out to be a very beautiful orchid indeed. How busy I shall be to-morrow! I must see to-night just exactly what to do with these things, and to-morrow I shall set to work."

"They found poor Batten lying dead, or dying, in a mangrove swamp—I forget which," he began again presently, "with one of these very orchids crushed up under his body. He had been unwell for some days with some kind of native fever, and I suppose he fainted. These mangrove swamps are very unwholesome. Every drop of blood, they say, was taken out of him by the jungle-leeches. It may be that very plant that cost him his life to obtain."

"I think none the better of it for that."

"Men must work though women may weep," said Wedderburn with profound gravity.

"Fancy dying away from every comfort in a nasty swamp! Fancy being ill of fever with nothing to take but chlorodyne and quinine—if men were left to themselves they would live on chlorodyne and quinine—and no one round you but horrible natives! They say the Andaman islanders are most disgusting wretches—and, anyhow, they can scarcely make good nurses, not having the necessary training. And just for people in England to have orchids!"

"I don't suppose it was comfortable, but some men seem to enjoy that kind of thing," said Wedderburn. "Anyhow, the natives of his party were sufficiently civilised to take care of all his collection until his colleague, who was an ornithologist, came back again from the interior; though they could not tell the species of the orchid, and had let it wither. And it makes these things more interesting."

"It makes them disgusting. I should be afraid of some of the malaria clinging to them. And just think, there has been a dead body lying across that ugly thing! I never thought of that before. There! I declare I cannot eat another mouthful of dinner."

"I will take them off the table if you like, and put them in the window-seat. I can see them just as well there."

The next few days he was indeed singularly busy in his steamy little hothouse, fussing about with charcoal, lumps of teak, moss, and all the other mysteries of the orchid cultivator. He considered he was having a wonderfully eventful time. In the evening he would talk about these new orchids to his friends, and over and over again he reverted to his expectation of something strange.

Several of the Vandas and the Dendrobium died under his care, but presently the strange orchid began to show signs of life. He was delighted, and took his housekeeper right away from jam-making to see it at once, directly he made the discovery.

"That is a bud," he said, "and presently there will be a lot of leaves there, and those little things coming out here are aerial rootlets."

"They look to me like little white fingers poking out of the brown," said his housekeeper. "I don't like them."

"Why not?"

"I don't know. They look like fingers trying to get at you. I can't help my likes and dislikes."

"I don't know for certain, but I don't think there are any orchids I know that have aerial rootlets quite like that. It may be my fancy, of course. You see they are a little flattened at the ends."

"I don't like 'em," said his housekeeper, suddenly shivering and turning away. "I know it's very silly of me—and I'm very sorry, particularly as you like the thing so much. But I can't help thinking of that corpse."

"But it may not be that particular plant. That was merely a guess of mine."

His housekeeper shrugged her shoulders. "Anyhow I don't like it," she said.

Wedderburn felt a little hurt at her dislike to the plant. But that did not prevent his talking to her about orchids generally, and this orchid in particular, whenever he felt inclined.

"There are such queer things about orchids," he said one day; "such possibilities of surprises. You know, Darwin studied their fertilisation, and showed that the whole structure of an ordinary orchid flower was contrived in order that moths might carry the pollen from plant to plant. Well, it seems that there are lots of orchids known the flower of which cannot possibly be used for fertilisation in that way. Some of the Cypripediums, for instance; there are no insects known that can possibly fertilise them, and some of them have never been found with seed."

"But how do they form new plants?"

"By runners and tubers, and that kind of outgrowth. That is easily explained. The puzzle is, what are the flowers for?

"Very likely," he added, "my orchid may be something extraordinary in that way. If so I shall study it. I have often thought of making researches as Darwin did. But hitherto I have not found the time, or something else has happened to prevent it. The leaves are beginning to unfold now. I do wish you would come and see them!"

But she said that the orchid-house was so hot it gave her the headache. She had seen the plant once again, and the aerial rootlets, which were now some of them more than a foot long, had unfortunately reminded her of tentacles reaching out after something; and they got into her dreams, growing after her with incredible rapidity. So that she had settled to her entire satisfaction that she would not see that plant again, and Wedderburn had to admire its leaves alone. They were of the ordinary broad form, and a deep glossy green, with splashes and dots of deep red towards the base He knew of no other leaves quite like them. The plant was placed on a low bench near the thermometer, and close by was a simple arrangement by which a tap dripped on the hot-water pipes and kept the air steamy. And he spent his afternoons now with some regularity meditating on the approaching flowering of this strange plant.

And at last the great thing happened. Directly he entered the little glass house he knew that the spike had burst out, although his great Paloeonophis Lowii hid the corner where his new darling stood. There was a new odour in the air, a rich, intensely sweet scent, that overpowered every other in that crowded, steaming little greenhouse.

Directly he noticed this he hurried down to the strange orchid. And, behold! the trailing green spikes bore now three great splashes of blossom, from which this overpowering sweetness proceeded. He stopped before them in an ecstasy of admiration.

The flowers were white, with streaks of golden orange upon the petals; the heavy labellum was coiled into an intricate projection, and a wonderful bluish purple mingled there with the gold. He could see at once that the genus was altogether a new one. And the insufferable scent! How hot the place was! The blossoms swam before his eyes.

He would see if the temperature was right. He made a step towards the thermometer. Suddenly everything appeared unsteady. The bricks on the floor were dancing up and down. Then the white blossoms, the green leaves behind them, the whole greenhouse, seemed to sweep sideways, and then in a curve upward.

* * * * *

At half-past four his cousin made the tea, according to their invariable custom. But Wedderburn did not come in for his tea.

"He is worshipping that horrid orchid," she told herself, and waited ten minutes. "His watch must have stopped. I will go and call him."

She went straight to the hothouse, and, opening the door, called his name. There was no reply. She noticed that the air was very close, and loaded with an intense perfume. Then she saw something lying on the bricks between the hot-water pipes.

For a minute, perhaps, she stood motionless.

He was lying, face upward, at the foot of the strange orchid. The tentacle-like aerial rootlets no longer swayed freely in the air, but were crowded together, a tangle of grey ropes, and stretched tight, with their ends closely applied to his chin and neck and hands.

She did not understand. Then she saw from under one of the exultant tentacles upon his cheek there trickled a little thread of blood.

With an inarticulate cry she ran towards him, and tried to pull him away from the leech-like suckers. She snapped two of these tentacles, and their sap dripped red.

Then the overpowering scent of the blossom began to make her head reel. How they clung to him! She tore at the tough ropes, and he and the white inflorescence swam about her. She felt she was fainting, knew she must not. She left him and hastily opened the nearest door, and, after she had panted for a moment in the fresh air, she had a brilliant inspiration. She caught up a flower-pot and smashed in the windows at the end of the greenhouse. Then she re-entered. She tugged now with renewed strength at Wedderburn's motionless body, and brought the strange orchid crashing to the floor. It still clung with the grimmest tenacity to its victim. In a frenzy, she lugged it and him into the open air.

Then she thought of tearing through the sucker rootlets one by one, and in another minute she had released him and was dragging him away from the horror.

He was white and bleeding from a dozen circular patches.

The odd-job man was coming up the garden, amazed at the smashing of glass, and saw her emerge, hauling the inanimate body with red-stained hands. For a moment he thought impossible things.

"Bring some water!" she cried, and her voice dispelled his fancies. When, with unnatural alacrity, he returned with the water, he found her weeping with excitement, and with Wedderburn's head upon her knee, wiping the blood from his face.

"What's the matter?" said Wedderburn, opening his eyes feebly, and closing them again at once.

"Go and tell Annie to come out here to me, and then go for Dr. Haddon at once," she said to the odd-job man so soon as he brought the water; and added, seeing he hesitated, "I will tell you all about it when you come back."

Presently Wedderburn opened his eyes again, and, seeing that he was troubled by the puzzle of his position, she explained to him, "You fainted in the hothouse."

"And the orchid?"

"I will see to that," she said.

Wedderburn had lost a good deal of blood, but beyond that he had suffered no very great injury. They gave him brandy mixed with some pink extract of meat, and carried him upstairs to bed. His housekeeper told her incredible story in fragments to Dr. Haddon. "Come to the orchid-house and see," she said.

The cold outer air was blowing in through the open door, and the sickly perfume was almost dispelled. Most of the torn aerial rootlets lay already withered amidst a number of dark stains upon the bricks. The stem of the inflorescence was broken by the fall of the plant, and the flowers were growing limp and brown at the edges of the petals. The doctor stooped towards it, then saw that one of the aerial rootlets still stirred feebly, and hesitated.

The next morning the strange orchid still lay there, black now and putrescent. The door banged intermittently in the morning breeze, and all the array of Wedderburn's orchids was shrivelled and prostrate. But Wedderburn himself was bright and garrulous upstairs in the glory of his strange adventure.

V.

IN THE AVU OBSERVATORY.

The observatory at Avu, in Borneo, stands on the spur of the mountain. To the north rises the old crater, black at night against the unfathomable blue of the sky. From the little circular building, with its mushroom dome, the slopes plunge steeply downward into the black mysteries of the tropical forest beneath. The little house in which the observer and his assistant live is about fifty yards from the observatory, and beyond this are the huts of their native attendants.

Thaddy, the chief observer, was down with a slight fever. His assistant, Woodhouse, paused for a moment in silent contemplation of the tropical night before commencing his solitary vigil. The night was very still. Now and then voices and laughter came from the native huts, or the cry of some strange animal was heard from the midst of the mystery of the forest. Nocturnal insects appeared in ghostly fashion out of the darkness, and fluttered round his light. He thought, perhaps, of all the possibilities of discovery that still lay in the black tangle beneath him; for to the naturalist the virgin forests of Borneo are still a wonderland full of strange questions and half-suspected discoveries. Woodhouse carried a small lantern in his hand, and its yellow glow contrasted vividly with the infinite series of tints between lavender-blue and black in which the landscape was painted. His hands and face were smeared with ointment against the attacks of the mosquitoes.

Even in these days of celestial photography, work done in a purely temporary erection, and with only the most primitive appliances in addition to the telescope, still involves a very large amount of cramped and motionless watching. He sighed as he thought of the physical fatigues before him, stretched himself, and entered the observatory.

The reader is probably familiar with the structure of an ordinary astronomical observatory. The building is usually cylindrical in shape, with a very light hemispherical roof capable of being turned round from the interior. The telescope is supported upon a stone pillar in the centre, and a clockwork arrangement compensates for the earth's rotation, and allows a star once found to be continuously observed. Besides this, there is a compact tracery of wheels and screws about its point of support, by which the astronomer adjusts it. There is, of course, a slit in the movable roof which follows the eye of the telescope in its survey of the heavens. The observer sits or lies on a sloping wooden arrangement, which he can wheel to any part of the observatory as the position of the telescope may require. Within it is advisable to have things as dark as possible, in order to enhance the brilliance of the stars observed.

The lantern flared as Woodhouse entered his circular den, and the general darkness fled into black shadows behind the big machine, from which it presently seemed to creep back over the whole place again as the light waned. The slit was a profound transparent blue, in which six stars shone with tropical brilliance, and their light lay, a pallid gleam, along the black tube of the instrument. Woodhouse shifted the roof, and then proceeding to the telescope, turned first one wheel and then another, the great cylinder slowly swinging into a new position. Then he glanced through the finder, the little companion telescope, moved the roof a little more, made some further adjustments, and set the clockwork in motion. He took off his jacket, for the night was very hot, and pushed into position the uncomfortable seat to which he was condemned for the next four hours. Then with a sigh he resigned himself to his watch upon the mysteries of space.

There was no sound now in the observatory, and the lantern waned steadily. Outside there was the occasional cry of some animal in alarm or pain, or calling to its mate, and the intermittent sounds of the Malay and Dyak servants. Presently one of the men began a queer chanting song, in which the others joined at intervals. After this it would seem that they turned in for the night, for no further sound came from their direction, and the whispering stillness became more and more profound.

The clockwork ticked steadily. The shrill hum of a mosquito explored the place and grew shriller in indignation at Woodhouse's ointment. Then the lantern went out and all the observatory was black.

Woodhouse shifted his position presently, when the slow movement of the telescope had carried it beyond the limits of his comfort.

He was watching a little group of stars in the Milky Way, in one of which his chief had seen or fancied a remarkable colour variability. It was not a part of the regular work for which the establishment existed, and for that reason perhaps Woodhouse was deeply interested. He must have forgotten things terrestrial. All his attention was concentrated upon the great blue circle of the telescope field—a circle powdered, so it seemed, with an innumerable multitude of stars, and all luminous against the blackness of its setting. As he watched he seemed to himself to become incorporeal, as if he too were floating in the ether of space. Infinitely remote was the faint red spot he was observing.

Suddenly the stars were blotted out. A flash of blackness passed, and they were visible again.

"Queer," said Woodhouse. "Must have been a bird."

The thing happened again, and immediately after the great tube shivered as though it had been struck. Then the dome of the observatory resounded with a series of thundering blows. The stars seemed to sweep aside as the telescope—which had been unclamped—swung round and away from the slit in the roof.

"Great Scott!" cried Woodhouse. "What's this?"

Some huge vague black shape, with a flapping something like a wing, seemed to be struggling in the aperture of the roof. In another moment the slit was clear again, and the luminous haze of the Milky Way shone warm and bright.

The interior of the roof was perfectly black, and only a scraping sound marked the whereabouts of the unknown creature.

Woodhouse had scrambled from the seat to his feet. He was trembling violently and in a perspiration with the suddenness of the occurrence. Was the thing, whatever it was, inside or out? It was big, whatever else it might be. Something shot across the skylight, and the telescope swayed. He started violently and put his arm up. It was in the observatory, then, with him. It was clinging to the roof apparently. What the devil was it? Could it see him?

He stood for perhaps a minute in a state of stupefaction. The beast, whatever it was, clawed at the interior of the dome, and then something flapped almost into his face, and he saw the momentary gleam of starlight on a skin like oiled leather. His water-bottle was knocked off his little table with a smash.

The sense of some strange bird-creature hovering a few yards from his face in the darkness was indescribably unpleasant to Woodhouse. As his thought returned he concluded that it must be some night-bird or large bat. At any risk he would see what it was, and pulling a match from his pocket, he tried to strike it on the telescope seat. There was a smoking streak of phosphorescent light, the match flared for a moment, and he saw a vast wing sweeping towards him, a gleam of grey-brown fur, and then he was struck in the face and the match knocked out of his hand. The blow was aimed at his temple, and a claw tore sideways down to his cheek. He reeled and fell, and he heard the extinguished lantern smash. Another blow followed as he fell. He was partly stunned, he felt his own warm blood stream out upon his face. Instinctively he felt his eyes had been struck at, and, turning over on his face to save them, tried to crawl under the protection of the telescope.

He was struck again upon the back, and he heard his jacket rip, and then the thing hit the roof of the observatory. He edged as far as he could between the wooden seat and the eyepiece of the instrument, and turned his body round so that it was chiefly his feet that were exposed. With these he could at least kick. He was still in a mystified state. The strange beast banged about in the darkness, and presently clung to the telescope, making it sway and the gear rattle. Once it flapped near him, and he kicked out madly and felt a soft body with his feet. He was horribly scared now. It must be a big thing to swing the telescope like that. He saw for a moment the outline of a head black against the starlight, with sharply-pointed upstanding ears and a crest between them. It seemed to him to be as big as a mastiff's. Then he began to bawl out as loudly as he could for help.

At that the thing came down upon him again. As it did so his hand touched something beside him on the floor. He kicked out, and the next moment his ankle was gripped and held by a row of keen teeth. He yelled again, and tried to free his leg by kicking with the other. Then he realised he had the broken water-bottle at his hand, and, snatching it, he struggled into a sitting posture, and feeling in the darkness towards his foot, gripped a velvety ear, like the ear of a big cat. He had seized the water-bottle by its neck and brought it down with a shivering crash upon the head of the strange beast. He repeated the blow, and then stabbed and jabbed with the jagged end of it, in the darkness, where he judged the face might be.

The small teeth relaxed their hold, and at once Woodhouse pulled his leg free and kicked hard. He felt the sickening feel of fur and bone giving under his boot. There was a tearing bite at his arm, and he struck over it at the face, as he judged, and hit damp fur.

There was a pause; then he heard the sound of claws; and the dragging of a heavy body away from him over the observatory floor. Then there was silence, broken only by his own sobbing breathing, and a sound like licking. Everything was black except the parallelogram of the blue skylight with the luminous dust of stars, against which the end of the telescope now appeared in silhouette. He waited, as it seemed, an interminable time.

Was the thing coming on again? He felt in his trouser-pocket for some matches, and found one remaining. He tried to strike this, but the floor was wet, and it spat and went out. He cursed. He could not see where the door was situated. In his struggle he had quite lost his bearings. The strange beast, disturbed by the splutter of the match, began to move again. "Time!" called Woodhouse, with a sudden gleam of mirth, but the thing was not coming at him again. He must have hurt it, he thought, with the broken bottle. He felt a dull pain in his ankle. Probably he was bleeding there. He wondered if it would support him if he tried to stand up. The night outside was very still. There was no sound of any one moving. The sleepy fools had not heard those wings battering upon the dome, nor his shouts. It was no good wasting strength in shouting. The monster flapped its wings and startled him into a defensive attitude. He hit his elbow against the seat, and it fell over with a crash. He cursed this, and then he cursed the darkness.

Suddenly the oblong patch of starlight seemed to sway to and fro. Was he going to faint? It would never do to faint. He clenched his fists and set his teeth to hold himself together. Where had the door got to? It occurred to him he could get his bearings by the stars visible through the skylight. The patch of stars he saw was in Sagittarius and south-eastward; the door was north—or was it north by west? He tried to think. If he could get the door open he might retreat. It might be the thing was wounded. The suspense was beastly. "Look here!" he said, "if you don't come on, I shall come at you."

Then the thing began clambering up the side of the observatory, and he saw its black outline gradually blot out the skylight. Was it in retreat? He forgot about the door, and watched as the dome shifted and creaked. Somehow he did not feel very frightened or excited now. He felt a curious sinking sensation inside him. The sharply-defined patch of light, with the black form moving across it, seemed to be growing smaller and smaller. That was curious. He began to feel very thirsty, and yet he did not feel inclined to get anything to drink. He seemed to be sliding down a long funnel.

He felt a burning sensation in his throat, and then he perceived it was broad daylight, and that one of the Dyak servants was looking at him with a curious expression. Then there was the top of Thaddy's face upside down. Funny fellow, Thaddy, to go about like that! Then he grasped the situation better, and perceived that his head was on Thaddy's knee, and Thaddy was giving him brandy. And then he saw the eyepiece of the telescope with a lot of red smears on it. He began to remember.

"You've made this observatory in a pretty mess," said Thaddy.

The Dyak boy was beating up an egg in brandy. Woodhouse took this and sat up. He felt a sharp twinge of pain. His ankle was tied up, so were his arm and the side of his face. The smashed glass, red-stained, lay about the floor, the telescope seat was overturned, and by the opposite wall was a dark pool. The door was open, and he saw the grey summit of the mountain against a brilliant background of blue sky.

"Pah!" said Woodhouse. "Who's been killing calves here? Take me out of it."

Then he remembered the Thing, and the fight he had had with it.

"What was it?" he said to Thaddy—"the Thing I fought with?".

"You know that best," said Thaddy. "But, anyhow, don't worry yourself now about it. Have some more to drink."

Thaddy, however, was curious enough, and it was a hard struggle between duty and inclination to keep Woodhouse quiet until he was decently put away in bed, and had slept upon the copious dose of meat extract Thaddy considered advisable. They then talked it over together.

"It was," said Woodhouse, "more like a big bat than anything else in the world. It had sharp, short ears, and soft fur, and its wings were leathery. Its teeth were little but devilish sharp, and its jaw could not have been very strong or else it would have bitten through my ankle."

"It has pretty nearly," said Thaddy.

"It seemed to me to hit out with its claws pretty freely. That is about as much as I know about the beast. Our conversation was intimate, so to speak, and yet not confidential."

"The Dyak chaps talk about a Big Colugo, a Klang-utang—whatever that may be. It does not often attack man, but I suppose you made it nervous. They say there is a Big Colugo and a Little Colugo, and a something else that sounds like gobble. They all fly about at night. For my own part, I know there are flying foxes and flying lemurs about here, but they are none of them very big beasts."

"There are more things in heaven and earth," said Woodhouse—and Thaddy groaned at the quotation—"and more particularly in the forests of Borneo, than are dreamt of in our philosophies. On the whole, if the Borneo fauna is going to disgorge any more of its novelties upon me, I should prefer that it did so when I was not occupied in the observatory at night and alone."

VI.

AEPYORNIS ISLAND.

The man with the scarred face leant over the table and looked at my bundle.

"Orchids?" he asked.

"A few," I said.

"Cypripediums," he said.

"Chiefly," said I.

"Anything new? I thought not. I did these islands twenty-five—twenty-seven years ago. If you find anything new here—well, it's brand new. I didn't leave much."

"I'm not a collector," said I.

"I was young then," he went on. "Lord! how I used to fly round." He seemed to take my measure. "I was in the East Indies two years, and in Brazil seven. Then I went to Madagascar."

"I know a few explorers by name," I said, anticipating a yarn. "Whom did you collect for?"

"Dawson's. I wonder if you've heard the name of Butcher ever?"

"Butcher—Butcher?" The name seemed vaguely present in my memory; then I recalled Butcher v. Dawson. "Why!" said I, "you are the man who sued them for four years' salary—got cast away on a desert island..."

"Your servant," said the man with the scar, bowing. "Funny case, wasn't it? Here was me, making a little fortune on that island, doing nothing for it neither, and them quite unable to give me notice. It often used to amuse me thinking over it while I was there. I did calculations of it—big—all over the blessed atoll in ornamental figuring."

"How did it happen?" said I. "I don't rightly remember the case."

"Well... You've heard of the AEpyornis?"

"Rather. Andrews was telling me of a new species he was working on only a month or so ago. Just before I sailed. They've got a thigh bone, it seems, nearly a yard long. Monster the thing must have been!"

"I believe you," said the man with the scar. "It was a monster. Sindbad's roc was just a legend of 'em. But when did they find these bones?"

"Three or four years ago—'91, I fancy. Why?"

"Why? Because I found them—Lord!—it's nearly twenty years ago. If Dawson's hadn't been silly about that salary they might have made a perfect ring in 'em... I couldn't help the infernal boat going adrift."

He paused. "I suppose it's the same place. A kind of swamp about ninety miles north of Antananarivo. Do you happen to know? You have to go to it along the coast by boats. You don't happen to remember, perhaps?"

"I don't. I fancy Andrews said something about a swamp."

"It must be the same. It's on the east coast. And somehow there's something in the water that keeps things from decaying. Like creosote it smells. It reminded me of Trinidad. Did they get any more eggs? Some of the eggs I found were a foot-and-a-half long. The swamp goes circling round, you know, and cuts off this bit. It's mostly salt, too. Well... What a time I had of it! I found the things quite by accident. We went for eggs, me and two native chaps, in one of those rum canoes all tied together, and found the bones at the same time. We had a tent and provisions for four days, and we pitched on one of the firmer places. To think of it brings that odd tarry smell back even now. It's funny work. You go probing into the mud with iron rods, you know. Usually the egg gets smashed. I wonder how long it is since these AEpyornises really lived. The missionaries say the natives have legends about when they were alive, but I never heard any such stories myself.[*] But certainly those eggs we got were as fresh as if they had been new laid. Fresh! Carrying them down to the boat one of my nigger chaps dropped one on a rock and it smashed. How I lammed into the beggar! But sweet it was, as if it was new laid, not even smelly, and its mother dead these four hundred years, perhaps. Said a centipede had bit him. However, I'm getting off the straight with the story. It had taken us all day to dig into the slush and get these eggs out unbroken, and we were all covered with beastly black mud, and naturally I was cross. So far as I knew they were the only eggs that have ever been got out not even cracked. I went afterwards to see the ones they have at the Natural History Museum in London; all of them were cracked and just stuck together like a mosaic, and bits missing. Mine were perfect, and I meant to blow them when I got back. Naturally I was annoyed at the silly duffer dropping three hours' work just on account of a centipede. I hit him about rather."

[Footnote *: No European is known to have seen a live AEpyornis, with the doubtful exception of MacAndrew, who visited Madagascar in 1745.—H.G.W.]

The man with the scar took out a clay pipe. I placed my pouch before him.

He filled up absent-mindedly.

"How about the others? Did you get those home? I don't remember—"

"That's the queer part of the story. I had three others. Perfectly fresh eggs. Well, we put 'em in the boat, and then I went up to the tent to make some coffee, leaving my two heathens down by the beach—the one fooling about with his sting and the other helping him. It never occurred to me that the beggars would take advantage of the peculiar position I was in to pick a quarrel. But I suppose the centipede poison and the kicking I had given him had upset the one—he was always a cantankerous sort—and he persuaded the other.

"I remember I was sitting and smoking and boiling up the water over a spirit-lamp business I used to take on these expeditions. Incidentally I was admiring the swamp under the sunset. All black and blood-red it was, in streaks—a beautiful sight. And up beyond the land rose grey and hazy to the hills, and the sky behind them red, like a furnace mouth. And fifty yards behind the back of me was these blessed heathen—quite regardless of the tranquil air of things—plotting to cut off with the boat and leave me all alone with three days' provisions and a canvas tent, and nothing to drink whatsoever beyond a little keg of water. I heard a kind of yelp behind me, and there they were in this canoe affair—it wasn't properly a boat—and, perhaps, twenty yards from land. I realised what was up in a moment. My gun was in the tent, and, besides, I had no bullets—only duck shot. They knew that. But I had a little revolver in my pocket, and I pulled that out as I ran down to the beach.

"'Come back!' says I, flourishing it.

"They jabbered something at me, and the man that broke the egg jeered. I aimed at the other—because he was unwounded and had the paddle, and I missed. They laughed. However, I wasn't beat. I knew I had to keep cool, and I tried him again and made him jump with the whang of it. He didn't laugh that time. The third time I got his head, and over he went, and the paddle with him. It was a precious lucky shot for a revolver. I reckon it was fifty yards. He went right under. I don't know if he was shot, or simply stunned and drowned. Then I began to shout to the other chap to come back, but he huddled up in the canoe and refused to answer. So I fired out my revolver at him and never got near him.

"I felt a precious fool, I can tell you. There I was on this rotten, black beach, flat swamp all behind me, and the flat sea, cold after the sun set, and just this black canoe drifting steadily out to sea. I tell you I damned Dawson's and Jamrach's and

Museums and all the rest of it just to rights. I bawled to this nigger to come back, until my voice went up into a scream.

"There was nothing for it but to swim after him and take my luck with the sharks. So I opened my clasp-knife and put it in my mouth, and took off my clothes and waded in. As soon as I was in the water I lost sight of the canoe, but I aimed, as I judged, to head it off. I hoped the man in it was too bad to navigate it, and that it would keep on drifting in the same direction. Presently it came up over the horizon again to the south-westward about. The afterglow of sunset was well over now and the dim of night creeping up. The stars were coming through the blue. I swum like a champion, though my legs and arms were soon aching.

"However, I came up to him by the time the stars were fairly out. As it got darker I began to see all manner of glowing things in the water— phosphorescence, you know. At times it made me giddy. I hardly knew which was stars and which was phosphorescence, and whether I was swimming on my head or my heels. The canoe was as black as sin, and the ripple under the bows like liquid fire. I was naturally chary of clambering up into it. I was anxious to see what he was up to first. He seemed to be lying cuddled up in a lump in the bows, and the stern was all out of water. The thing kept turning round slowly as it drifted—-kind of waltzing, don't you know. I went to the stern and pulled it down, expecting him to wake up. Then I began to clamber in with my knife in my hand, and ready for a rush. But he never stirred. So there I sat in the stern of the little canoe, drifting away over the calm phosphorescent sea, and with all the host of the stars above me, waiting for something to happen.

"After a long time I called him by name, but he never answered. I was too tired to take any risks by going along to him. So we sat there. I fancy I dozed once or twice. When the dawn came I saw he was as dead as a doornail and all puffed up and purple. My three eggs and the bones were lying in the middle of the canoe, and the keg of water and some coffee and biscuits wrapped in a Cape Argus by his feet, and a tin of methylated spirit underneath him. There was no paddle, nor, in fact, anything except the spirit-tin that I could use as one, so I settled to drift until I was picked up. I held an inquest on him, brought in a verdict against some snake, scorpion, or centipede unknown, and sent him overboard.

"After that I had a drink of water and a few biscuits, and took a look round. I suppose a man low down as I was don't see very far; leastways, Madagascar was clean out of sight, and any trace of land at all. I saw a sail going south-westward—looked like a schooner but her hull never came up. Presently the sun got high in the sky and began to beat down upon me. Lord! it pretty near made my brains boil. I tried dipping my head in the sea, but after a while my eye fell on the Cape Argus, and I lay down flat in the canoe and spread this over me. Wonderful things these newspapers! I never read one through thoroughly before, but it's odd what you get up to when you're alone, as I was. I suppose I read that blessed old Cape Argus twenty times. The pitch in the canoe simply reeked with the heat and rose up into big blisters.

"I drifted ten days," said the man with the scar. "It's a little thing in the telling, isn't it? Every day was like the last. Except in the morning and the evening I never kept a look-out even—the blaze was so infernal. I didn't see a sail after the first three days, and those I saw took no notice of me. About the sixth night a ship went by scarcely half a mile away from me, with all its lights ablaze and its ports open, looking like a big firefly. There was music aboard. I stood up and shouted and screamed at it. The second day I broached one of the AEpyornis eggs, scraped the shell away at the end bit by bit, and tried it, and I was glad to find it was good enough to eat. A bit flavoury—not bad, I mean—but with something of the taste of a duck's egg. There was a kind of circular patch, about six inches across, on one side of the yoke, and with streaks of blood and a white mark like a ladder in it that I thought queer, but I did not understand what this meant at the time, and I wasn't inclined to be particular. The egg lasted me three days, with biscuits and a drink of water. I chewed coffee berries too—invigorating stuff. The second egg I opened about the eighth day, and it scared me."

The man with the scar paused. "Yes," he said, "developing."

"I daresay you find it hard to believe. I did, with the thing before me. There the egg had been, sunk in that cold black mud, perhaps three hundred years. But there was no mistaking it. There was the—what is it?—embryo, with its big head and curved back, and its heart beating under its throat, and the yolk shrivelled up and great membranes spreading inside of the shell and all over the yolk. Here was I hatching out the eggs of the biggest of all extinct birds, in a little canoe in the midst of the Indian Ocean. If old Dawson had known that! It was worth four years' salary. What do you think?

"However, I had to eat that precious thing up, every bit of it, before I sighted the reef, and some of the mouthfuls were beastly unpleasant. I left the third one alone. I held it up to the light, but the shell was too thick for me to get any notion of what might be happening inside; and though I fancied I heard blood pulsing, it might have been the rustle in my own ears, like what you listen to in a seashell.

"Then came the atoll. Came out of the sunrise, as it were, suddenly, close up to me. I drifted straight towards it until I was about half a mile from shore, not more, and then the current took a turn, and I had to paddle as hard as I could with my hands and bits of the AEpyornis shell to make the place. However, I got there. It was just a common atoll about four miles round, with a few trees growing and a spring in one place, and the lagoon full of parrot-fish. I took the egg ashore and put it in a good place, well above the tide lines and in the sun, to give it all the chance I could, and pulled the canoe up safe, and loafed about prospecting. It's rum how dull an atoll is. As soon as I had found a spring all the interest seemed to vanish. When I was a kid I thought nothing could be finer or more adventurous than the Robinson Crusoe business, but that place was as monotonous as a book of sermons. I went round finding eatable things and generally thinking; but I tell you I was bored to death before the first day was out. It shows my luck—the very day I landed the weather changed. A thunderstorm went by to the north and flicked its wing over the island, and in the night there came a drencher and a howling wind slap over us. It wouldn't have taken much, you know, to upset that canoe.

"I was sleeping under the canoe, and the egg was luckily among the sand higher up the beach, and the first thing I remember was a sound like a hundred pebbles hitting the boat at once, and a rush of water over my body. I'd been dreaming of Antananarivo, and I sat up and holloaed to Intoshi to ask her what the devil was up, and clawed out at the chair where the matches used to be. Then I remembered where I was. There were phosphorescent waves rolling up as if they meant to eat me, and all the rest of the night as black as pitch. The air was simply yelling. The clouds seemed down on your head almost, and the rain fell as if heaven was sinking and they were baling out the waters above the firmament. One great roller came writhing at me, like a fiery serpent, and I bolted. Then I thought of the canoe, and ran down to it as the water went hissing back again; but the thing had gone. I wondered about the egg then, and felt my way to it. It was all right and well out of reach of the maddest waves, so I sat down beside it and cuddled it for company. Lord! what a night that was!

"The storm was over before the morning. There wasn't a rag of cloud left in the sky when the dawn came, and all along the beach there were bits of plank scattered—which was the disarticulated skeleton, so to speak, of my canoe. However, that gave me something to do, for, taking advantage of two of the trees being together, I rigged up a kind of storm-shelter with these vestiges. And that day the egg hatched.

"Hatched, sir, when my head was pillowed on it and I was asleep. I heard a whack and felt a jar and sat up, and there was the end of the egg pecked out and a rum little brown head looking out at me. 'Lord!' I said, 'you're welcome'; and with a little difficulty he came out.

"He was a nice friendly little chap at first, about the size of a small hen—very much like most other young birds, only bigger. His plumage was a dirty brown to begin with, with a sort of grey scab that fell off it very soon, and scarcely feathers—a kind of downy hair. I can hardly express how pleased I was to see him. I tell you, Robinson Crusoe don't make near enough of his loneliness. But here was interesting company. He looked at me and winked his eye from the front backwards, like a hen, and gave a chirp and began to peck about at once, as though being hatched three hundred years too late was just nothing. 'Glad to see you, Man Friday!' says I, for I had naturally settled he was to be called Man Friday if ever he was hatched, as soon as ever I found the egg in the canoe had developed. I was a bit anxious about his feed, so I gave him a lump of raw parrot-fish at once. He took it, and opened his beak for more. I was glad of that for, under the circumstances, if he'd been at all fanciful, I should have had to eat him after all.

"You'd be surprised what an interesting bird that AEpyornis chick was. He followed me about from the very beginning. He used to stand by me and watch while I fished in the lagoon, and go shares in anything I caught. And he was sensible, too. There were nasty green warty things, like pickled gherkins, used to lie about on the beach, and he tried one of these and it upset him. He never even looked at any of them again.

"And he grew. You could almost see him grow. And as I was never much of a society man, his quiet, friendly ways suited me to a T. For nearly two years we were as happy as we could be on that island. I had no business worries, for I knew my salary was mounting up at Dawsons'. We would see a sail now and then, but nothing ever came near us. I amused myself, too, by decorating the island with designs worked in sea-urchins and fancy shells of various kinds. I put AEPYORNIS ISLAND all round the place very nearly, in big letters, like what you see done with coloured stones at railway stations in the old country, and mathematical calculations and drawings of various sorts. And I used to lie watching the blessed bird stalking round and growing, growing; and think how I could make a living out of him by showing him about if I ever got taken off. After his first moult he began to get handsome, with a crest and a blue wattle, and a lot of green feathers at the behind of him. And then I used to puzzle whether Dawsons' had any right to claim him or not. Stormy weather and in the rainy season we lay snug under the shelter I had made out of the old canoe, and I used to tell him lies about my friends at home. And after a storm we would go round the island together to see if there was any drift. It was a kind of idyll, you might say. If only I had had some tobacco it would have been simply just like heaven.

"It was about the end of the second year our little paradise went wrong. Friday was then about fourteen feet high to the bill of him, with a big, broad head like the end of a pickaxe, and two huge brown eyes with yellow rims, set together like a man's—not out of sight of each other like a hen's. His plumage was fine—none of the half-mourning style of your ostrich—more like a cassowary as far as colour and texture go. And then it was he began to cock his comb at me and give himself airs, and show signs of a nasty temper ...

"At last came a time when my fishing had been rather unlucky, and he began to hang about me in a queer, meditative way. I thought he might have been eating sea-cucumbers or something, but it was really just discontent on his part. I was hungry too, and when at last I landed a fish I wanted it for myself. Tempers were short that morning on both sides. He pecked at it and grabbed it, and I gave him a whack on the head to make him leave go. And at that he went for me. Lord! ...

"He gave me this in the face." The man indicated his scar. "Then he kicked me. It was like a carthorse. I got up, and seeing he hadn't finished, I started off full tilt with my arms doubled up over my face. But he ran on those gawky legs of his faster than a racehorse, and kept landing out at me with sledgehammer kicks, and bringing his pickaxe down on the back of my head. I made for the lagoon, and went in up to my neck. He stopped at the water, for he hated getting his feet wet, and began to make a shindy, something like a peacock's, only hoarser. He started strutting up and down the beach. I'll admit I felt small to see this blessed fossil lording it there. And my head and face were all bleeding, and—well, my body just one jelly of bruises.

"I decided to swim across the lagoon and leave him alone for a bit, until the affair blew over. I shinned up the tallest palm-tree, and sat there thinking of it all. I don't suppose I ever felt so hurt by anything before or since. It was the brutal ingratitude of the creature. I'd been more than a brother to him. I'd hatched him, educated him. A great gawky, out-of-date bird! And me a human being—heir of the ages and all that.

"I thought after a time he'd begin to see things in that light himself, and feel a little sorry for his behaviour. I thought if I was to catch some nice little bits of fish, perhaps, and go to him presently in a casual kind of way, and offer them to him, he might do the sensible thing. It took me some time to learn how unforgiving and cantankerous an extinct bird can be. Malice!

"I won't tell you all the little devices I tried to get that bird round again, I simply can't. It makes my cheek burn with shame even now to think of the snubs and buffets I had from this infernal curiosity. I tried violence. I chucked lumps of coral at him from a safe distance, but he only swallowed them. I shied my open knife at him and almost lost it, though it was too big for him to swallow. I tried starving him out and struck fishing, but he took to picking along the beach at low water after worms, and rubbed along on that. Half my time I spent up to my neck in the lagoon, and the rest up the palm-trees. One of them was scarcely high enough, and when he caught me up it he had a regular Bank Holiday with the calves of my legs. It got unbearable. I don't know if you have ever tried sleeping up a palm-tree. It gave me the most horrible nightmares. Think of the shame of it, too! Here was this extinct animal mooning about my island like a sulky duke, and me not allowed to rest the sole of my foot on the place. I used to cry with weariness and vexation. I told him straight that I didn't mean to be chased about a desert island by any damned anachronisms. I told him to go and peck a navigator of his own age. But he only snapped his beak at me. Great ugly bird, all legs and neck!

"I shouldn't like to say how long that went on altogether. I'd have killed him sooner if I'd known how. However, I hit on a way of settling him at last. It is a South American dodge. I joined all my fishing-lines together with stems of seaweed and things, and made a stoutish string, perhaps twelve yards in length or more, and I fastened two lumps of coral rock to the ends of this. It took me some time to do, because every now and then I had to go into the lagoon or up a tree as the fancy took me. This I whirled rapidly round my head, and then let it go at him. The first time I missed, but the next time the string caught his legs beautifully, and wrapped round them again and again. Over he went. I threw it standing waist-deep in the lagoon, and as soon as he went down I was out of the water and sawing at his neck with my knife ...

"I don't like to think of that even now. I felt like a murderer while I did it, though my anger was hot against him. When I stood over him and saw him bleeding on the white sand, and his beautiful great legs and neck writhing in his last agony ... Pah!

"With that tragedy loneliness came upon me like a curse. Good Lord! you can't imagine how I missed that bird. I sat by his corpse and sorrowed over him, and shivered as I looked round the desolate, silent reef. I thought of what a jolly little bird he had been when he was hatched, and of a thousand pleasant tricks he had played before he went wrong. I thought if I'd only wounded him I might have nursed him round into a better understanding. If I'd had any means of digging into the coral rock I'd have buried him. I felt exactly as if he was human. As it was, I couldn't think of eating him, so I put him in the lagoon, and the little fishes picked him clean. I didn't even save the feathers. Then one day a chap cruising about in a yacht had a fancy to see if my atoll still existed.

"He didn't come a moment too soon, for I was about sick enough of the desolation of it, and only hesitating whether I should walk out into the sea and finish up the business that way, or fall back on the green things...

"I sold the bones to a man named Winslow—a dealer near the British Museum, and he says he sold them to old Havers. It seems Havers didn't understand they were extra large, and it was only after his death they attracted attention. They called 'em AEpyornis—what was it?"

"AEpyornis vastus," said I. "It's funny, the very thing was mentioned to me by a friend of mine. When they found an AEpyornis, with a thigh a yard long, they thought they had reached the top of the scale, and called him AEpyornis maximus. Then some one turned up another thigh-bone four feet six or more, and that they called AEpyornis Titan. Then your vastus was found after old Havers died, in his collection, and then a vastissimus turned up."

"Winslow was telling me as much," said the man with the scar. "If they get any more AEpyornises, he reckons some scientific swell will go and burst a blood-vessel. But it was a queer thing to happen to a man; wasn't it— altogether?"

VII.

THE REMARKABLE CASE OF DAVIDSON'S EYES.

I.

The transitory mental aberration of Sidney Davidson, remarkable enough in itself, is still more remarkable if Wade's explanation is to be credited. It sets one dreaming of the oddest possibilities of intercommunication in the future, of spending an intercalary five minutes on the other side of the world, or being watched in our most secret operations by unsuspected eyes. It happened that I was the immediate witness of Davidson's seizure, and so it falls naturally to me to put the story upon paper.

When I say that I was the immediate witness of his seizure, I mean that I was the first on the scene. The thing happened at the Harlow Technical College, just beyond the Highgate Archway. He was alone in the larger laboratory when the thing happened. I was in a smaller room, where the balances are, writing up some notes. The thunderstorm had completely upset my work, of course. It was just after one of the louder peals that

I thought I heard some glass smash in the other room. I stopped writing, and turned round to listen. For a moment I heard nothing; the hail was playing the devil's tattoo on the corrugated zinc of the roof. Then came another sound, a smash—no doubt of it this time. Something heavy had been knocked off the bench. I jumped up at once and went and opened the door leading into the big laboratory.

I was surprised to hear a queer sort of laugh, and saw Davidson standing unsteadily in the middle of the room, with a dazzled look on his face. My first impression was that he was drunk. He did not notice me. He was clawing out at something invisible a yard in front of his face. He put out his hand, slowly, rather hesitatingly, and then clutched nothing. "What's come to it?" he said. He held up his hands to his face, fingers spread out. "Great Scott!" he said. The thing happened three or four years ago, when every one swore by that personage. Then he began raising his feet clumsily, as though he had expected to find them glued to the floor.

"Davidson!" cried I. "What's the matter with you?" He turned round in my direction and looked about for me. He looked over me and at me and on either side of me, without the slightest sign of seeing me. "Waves," he said; "and a remarkably neat schooner. I'd swear that was Bellow's voice. Hullo!" He shouted suddenly at the top of his voice.

I thought he was up to some foolery. Then I saw littered about his feet the shattered remains of the best of our electrometers. "What's up, man?" said I. "You've smashed the electrometer!"

"Bellows again!" said he. "Friends left, if my hands are gone. Something about electrometers. Which way are you, Bellows?" He suddenly came staggering towards me. "The damned stuff cuts like butter," he said. He walked straight into the bench and recoiled. "None so buttery that!" he said, and stood swaying.

I felt scared. "Davidson," said I, "what on earth's come over you?"

He looked round him in every direction. "I could swear that was Bellows.

Why don't you show yourself like a man, Bellows?"

It occurred to me that he must be suddenly struck blind. I walked round the table and laid my hand upon his arm. I never saw a man more startled in my life. He jumped away from me, and came round into an attitude of self-defence, his face fairly distorted with terror. "Good God!" he cried. "What was that?"

"It's I—Bellows. Confound it, Davidson!"

He jumped when I answered him and stared—how can I express it?—right through me. He began talking, not to me, but to himself. "Here in broad daylight on a clear beach. Not a place to hide in." He looked about him wildly. "Here! I'm off." He suddenly turned and ran headlong into the big electro-magnet—so violently that, as we found afterwards, he bruised his shoulder and jawbone cruelly. At that he stepped back a pace, and cried out with almost a whimper, "What, in Heaven's name, has come over me?" He stood, blanched with terror and trembling violently, with his right arm clutching his left, where that had collided with the magnet.

By that time I was excited and fairly scared. "Davidson," said I, "don't be afraid."

He was startled at my voice, but not so excessively as before. I repeated my words in as clear and as firm a tone as I could assume. "Bellows," he said, "is that you?"

"Can't you see it's me?"

He laughed. "I can't even see it's myself. Where the devil are we?"

"Here," said I, "in the laboratory."

"The laboratory!" he answered in a puzzled tone, and put his hand to his forehead. "I was in the laboratory—till that flash came, but I'm hanged if I'm there now. What ship is that?"

"There's no ship," said I. "Do be sensible, old chap."

"No ship!" he repeated, and seemed to forget my denial forthwith. "I suppose," said he slowly, "we're both dead. But the rummy part is I feel just as though I still had a body. Don't get used to it all at once, I suppose. The old shop was struck by lightning, I suppose. Jolly quick thing, Bellows—eigh?"

"Don't talk nonsense. You're very much alive. You are in the laboratory, blundering about. You've just smashed a new electrometer. I don't envy you when Boyce arrives."

He stared away from me towards the diagrams of cryohydrates. "I must be deaf," said he. "They've fired a gun, for there goes the puff of smoke, and I never heard a sound."

I put my hand on his arm again, and this time he was less alarmed. "We seem to have a sort of invisible bodies," said he. "By Jove! there's a boat coming round the headland. It's very much like the old life after all—in a different climate."

I shook his arm. "Davidson," I cried, "wake up!"

II.

It was just then that Boyce came in. So soon as he spoke Davidson exclaimed: "Old Boyce! Dead too! What a lark!" I hastened to explain that Davidson was in a kind of somnambulistic trance. Boyce was interested at once. We both did all we could to rouse the fellow out of his extraordinary state. He answered our questions, and asked us some of his own, but his attention seemed distracted by his hallucination about a beach and a ship. He kept interpolating observations concerning some boat and the davits, and sails filling with the wind. It made one feel queer, in the dusky laboratory, to hear him saying such things.

He was blind and helpless. We had to walk him down the passage, one at each elbow, to Boyce's private room, and while Boyce talked to him there, and humoured him about this ship idea, I went along the corridor and asked old Wade to come and look at him. The voice of our Dean sobered him a little, but not very much. He asked where his hands were, and why he had to walk about up to his waist in the ground. Wade thought over him a long time—you know how he knits his brows—and then made him feel the couch, guiding his hands to it. "That's a couch," said Wade. "The couch in the private room of Professor Boyce. Horse-hair stuffing."

Davidson felt about, and puzzled over it, and answered presently that he could feel it all right, but he couldn't see it.

"What do you see?" asked Wade. Davidson said he could see nothing but a lot of sand and broken-up shells. Wade gave him some other things to feel, telling him what they were, and watching him keenly.

"The ship is almost hull down," said Davidson presently, apropos of nothing.

"Never mind the ship," said Wade. "Listen to me, Davidson. Do you know what hallucination means?"

"Rather," said Davidson.

"Well, everything you see is hallucinatory."

"Bishop Berkeley," said Davidson.

"Don't mistake me," said Wade. "You are alive and in this room of Boyce's. But something has happened to your eyes. You cannot see; you can feel and hear, but not see. Do you follow me?"

"It seems to me that I see too much." Davidson rubbed his knuckles into his eyes. "Well?" he said.

"That's all. Don't let it perplex you. Bellows here and I will take you home in a cab."

"Wait a bit." Davidson thought. "Help me to sit down," said he presently; "and now—I'm sorry to trouble you—but will you tell me all that over again?"

Wade repeated it very patiently. Davidson shut his eyes, and pressed his hands upon his forehead. "Yes," said he. "It's quite right. Now my eyes are shut I know you're right. That's you, Bellows, sitting by me on the couch. I'm in England again. And we're in the dark."

Then he opened his eyes. "And there," said he, "is the sun just rising, and the yards of the ship, and a tumbled sea, and a couple of birds flying. I never saw anything so real. And I'm sitting up to my neck in a bank of sand."

He bent forward and covered his face with his hands. Then he opened his eyes again. "Dark sea and sunrise! And yet I'm sitting on a sofa in old Boyce's room!... God help me!"

III.

That was the beginning. For three weeks this strange affection of Davidson's eyes continued unabated. It was far worse than being blind. He was absolutely helpless, and had to be fed like a newly-hatched bird, and led about and undressed. If he attempted to move, he fell over things or struck himself against walls or doors. After a day or so he got used to hearing our voices without seeing us, and willingly admitted he was at home, and that Wade was right in what he told him. My sister, to whom he was engaged, insisted on coming to see him, and would sit for hours every day while he talked about this beach of his. Holding her hand seemed to comfort him immensely. He explained that when we left the College and drove home—he lived in Hampstead village—it appeared to him as if we drove right through a sandhill—it was perfectly black until he emerged again—and through rocks and trees and solid obstacles, and when he was taken to his own room it made him giddy and almost frantic with the fear of falling, because going upstairs seemed to lift him thirty or forty feet above the rocks of his imaginary island. He kept saying he should smash all the eggs. The end was that he had to be taken down into his father's consulting room and laid upon a couch that stood there.

He described the island as being a bleak kind of place on the whole, with very little vegetation, except some peaty stuff, and a lot of bare rock. There were multitudes of penguins, and they made the rocks white and disagreeable to see. The sea was often rough, and once there was a thunderstorm, and he lay and shouted at the silent flashes. Once or twice seals pulled up on the beach, but only on the first two or three days. He said it was very funny the way in which the penguins used to waddle right through him, and how he seemed to lie among them without disturbing them.

I remember one odd thing, and that was when he wanted very badly to smoke. We put a pipe in his hands—he almost poked his eye out with it—and lit it. But he couldn't taste anything. I've since found it's the same with me—I don't know if it's the usual case—that I cannot enjoy tobacco at all unless I can see the smoke.

But the queerest part of his vision came when Wade sent him out in a Bath-chair to get fresh air. The Davidsons hired a chair, and got that deaf and obstinate dependant of theirs, Widgery, to attend to it. Widgery's ideas of healthy expeditions were peculiar. My sister, who had been to the Dogs' Home, met them in Camden Town, towards King's Cross, Widgery trotting along complacently, and Davidson, evidently most distressed, trying in his feeble, blind way to attract Widgery's attention.

He positively wept when my sister spoke to him. "Oh, get me out of this horrible darkness!" he said, feeling for her hand. "I must get out of it, or I shall die." He was quite incapable of explaining what was the matter, but my sister decided he must go home, and presently, as they went uphill towards Hampstead, the horror seemed to drop from him. He said it was good to see the stars again, though it was then about noon and a blazing day.

"It seemed," he told me afterwards, "as if I was being carried irresistibly towards the water. I was not very much alarmed at first. Of course it was night there—a lovely night."

"Of course?" I asked, for that struck me as odd.

"Of course," said he. "It's always night there when it is day here... Well, we went right into the water, which was calm and shining under the moonlight—just a broad swell that seemed to grow broader and flatter as I came down into it. The surface glistened just like a skin—it might have been empty space underneath for all I could tell to the contrary. Very slowly, for I rode slanting into it, the water crept up to my eyes. Then I went under and the skin seemed to break and heal again about my eyes. The moon gave a jump up in the sky and grew green and dim, and fish, faintly glowing, came darting round me—and things that seemed made of luminous glass; and I passed through a tangle of seaweeds that shone with an oily lustre. And so I drove down into the sea, and the stars went out one by one, and the moon grew greener and darker, and the seaweed became a luminous purple-red. It was all very faint and mysterious, and everything seemed to quiver. And all the while I could hear the wheels of the Bath-chair creaking, and the footsteps of people going by, and a man in the distance selling the special Pall Mall.

"I kept sinking down deeper and deeper into the water. It became inky black about me, not a ray from above came down into that darkness, and the phosphorescent things grew brighter and brighter. The snaky branches of the deeper weeds flickered like the flames of spirit-lamps; but, after a time, there were no more weeds. The fishes came staring and gaping towards me, and into me and through me. I never imagined such fishes before. They had lines of fire along the sides of them as though they had been outlined with a luminous pencil. And there was a ghastly thing swimming backwards with a lot of twining arms. And then I saw, coming very slowly towards me through the gloom, a hazy mass of light that resolved itself as it drew nearer into multitudes of fishes, struggling and darting round something that drifted. I drove on straight towards it, and presently I saw in the midst of the tumult, and by the light of the fish, a bit of splintered spar looming over me, and a dark hull tilting over, and some glowing phosphorescent forms that were shaken and writhed as the fish bit at them. Then it was I began to try to attract Widgery's attention. A horror came upon me. Ugh! I should have driven right into those half-eaten—things. If your sister had not come! They had great holes in them, Bellows, and ... Never mind. But it was ghastly!"

IV.

For three weeks Davidson remained in this singular state, seeing what at the time we imagined was an altogether phantasmal world, and stone blind to the world around him. Then, one Tuesday, when I called I met old Davidson in the passage. "He can see his thumb!" the old gentleman said, in a perfect transport. He was struggling into his overcoat. "He can see his thumb, Bellows!" he said, with the tears in his eyes. "The lad will be all right yet."

I rushed in to Davidson. He was holding up a little book before his face, and looking at it and laughing in a weak kind of way.

"It's amazing," said he. "There's a kind of patch come there." He pointed with his finger. "I'm on the rocks as usual, and the penguins are staggering and flapping about as usual, and there's been a whale showing every now and then, but it's got too dark now to make him out. But put something there, and I see it—I do see it. It's very dim and broken in places, but I see it all the same, like a faint spectre of itself. I found it out this morning while they were dressing me. It's like a hole in this infernal phantom world. Just put your hand by mine. No—not there. Ah! Yes! I see it. The base of your thumb and a bit of cuff! It looks like the ghost of a bit of your hand sticking out of the darkling sky. Just by it there's a group of stars like a cross coming out."

From that time Davidson began to mend. His account of the change, like his account of the vision, was oddly convincing. Over patches of his field of vision, the phantom world grew fainter, grew transparent, as it were, and through these translucent gaps he began to see dimly the real world about him. The patches grew in size and number, ran together and spread until only here and there were blind spots left upon his eyes. He was able to get up and steer himself about, feed himself once more, read, smoke, and behave like an ordinary citizen again. At first it was very confusing to him to have these two pictures overlapping each other like the changing views of a lantern, but in a little while he began to distinguish the real from the illusory.

At first he was unfeignedly glad, and seemed only too anxious to complete his cure by taking exercise and tonics. But as that odd island of his began to fade away from him, he became queerly interested in it. He wanted particularly to go down into the deep sea again, and would spend half his time wandering about the low-lying parts of London, trying to find the water-logged wreck he had seen drifting. The glare of real daylight very soon impressed him so vividly as to blot out everything of his shadowy world, but of a night-time, in a darkened room, he could still see the white-splashed rocks of the island, and the clumsy penguins staggering to and fro. But even these grew fainter and fainter, and, at last, soon after he married my sister, he saw them for the last time.

V.

And now to tell of the queerest thing of all. About two years after his cure I dined with the Davidsons, and after dinner a man named Atkins called in. He is a lieutenant in the Royal Navy, and a pleasant, talkative man. He was on friendly terms with my brother-in-law, and was soon on friendly terms with me. It came out that he was engaged to Davidson's cousin, and incidentally he took out a kind of pocket photograph case to show us a new rendering of his fiancée. "And, by-the-by," said he, "here's the old Fulmar."

Davidson looked at it casually. Then suddenly his face lit up. "Good heavens!" said he. "I could almost swear——"

"What?" said Atkins.

"That I had seen that ship before."

"Don't see how you can have. She hasn't been out of the South Seas for six years, and before then——"

"But," began Davidson, and then, "Yes—that's the ship I dreamt of; I'm sure that's the ship I dreamt of. She was standing off an island that swarmed with penguins, and she fired a gun."

"Good Lord!" said Atkins, who had now heard the particulars of the seizure. "How the deuce could you dream that?"

And then, bit by bit, it came out that on the very day Davidson was seized, H.M.S. Fulmar had actually been off a little rock to the south of Antipodes Island. A boat had landed overnight to get penguins' eggs, had been delayed, and a thunderstorm drifting up, the boat's crew had waited until the morning before rejoining the ship. Atkins had been one of them, and he corroborated, word for word, the descriptions Davidson had given of the island and the boat. There is not the slightest doubt in any of our minds that Davidson has really seen the place. In some unaccountable way, while he moved hither and thither in London, his sight moved hither and thither in a manner that corresponded, about this distant island. How is absolutely a mystery.

That completes the remarkable story of Davidson's eyes. It's perhaps the best authenticated case in existence of real vision at a distance. Explanation there is none forthcoming, except what Professor Wade has thrown out. But his explanation invokes the Fourth Dimension, and a dissertation on theoretical kinds of space. To talk of there being "a kink in space" seems mere nonsense to me; it may be because I am no mathematician. When I said that nothing would alter the fact that the place is eight thousand miles away, he answered that two points might be a yard away on a sheet of paper, and yet be brought together by bending the paper round. The reader may grasp his argument, but I certainly do not. His idea seems to be that Davidson, stooping between the poles of the big electro-magnet, had some extraordinary twist given to his retinal elements through the sudden change in the field of force due to the lightning.

He thinks, as a consequence of this, that it may be possible to live visually in one part of the world, while one lives bodily in another. He has even made some experiments in support of his views; but, so far, he has simply succeeded in blinding a few dogs. I believe that is the net result of his work, though I have not seen him for some weeks. Latterly I have been so busy with my work in connection with the Saint Pancras installation that I have had little opportunity of calling to see him. But the whole of his theory seems fantastic to me. The facts concerning Davidson stand on an altogether different footing, and I can testify personally to the accuracy of every detail I have given.

VIII.

THE LORD OF THE DYNAMOS.

The chief attendant of the three dynamos that buzzed and rattled at Camberwell, and kept the electric railway going, came out of Yorkshire, and his name was James Holroyd. He was a practical electrician, but fond of whisky, a heavy, red-haired brute with irregular teeth. He doubted the existence of the Deity, but accepted Carnot's cycle, and he had read Shakespeare and found him weak in chemistry. His helper came out of the mysterious East, and his name was Azuma-zi. But Holroyd called him Pooh-bah. Holroyd liked a nigger help because he would stand kicking—a habit with Holroyd—and did not pry into the machinery and try to learn the ways of it. Certain odd possibilities of the negro mind brought into abrupt contact with the crown of our civilisation Holroyd never fully realised, though just at the end he got some inkling of them.

To define Azuma-zi was beyond ethnology. He was, perhaps, more negroid than anything else, though his hair was curly rather than frizzy, and his nose had a bridge. Moreover, his skin was brown rather than black, and the whites of his eyes were yellow. His broad cheekbones and narrow chin gave his face something of the viperine V. His head, too, was broad behind, and low and narrow at the forehead, as if his brain had been twisted round in the reverse way to a European's. He was short of stature and still shorter of English. In conversation he made numerous odd noises of no known marketable value, and his infrequent words were carved and wrought into heraldic grotesqueness. Holroyd tried to elucidate his religious beliefs, and—especially after whisky—lectured to him against superstition and missionaries. Azuma-zi, however, shirked the discussion of his gods, even though he was kicked for it.

Azuma-zi had come, clad in white but insufficient raiment, out of the stoke-hole of the Lord Clive, from the Straits Settlements and beyond, into London. He had heard even in his youth of the greatness and riches of London, where all the women are white and fair, and even the beggars in the streets are white, and he had arrived, with newly-earned gold coins in his pocket, to worship at the shrine of civilisation. The day of his landing was a dismal one; the sky was dun, and a wind-worried drizzle filtered down to the greasy streets, but he plunged boldly into the delights of Shadwell, and was presently cast up, shattered in health, civilised in costume, penniless, and, except in matters of the direst necessity, practically a dumb animal, to toil for James Holroyd, and to be bullied by him in the dynamo shed at Camberwell. And to James Holroyd bullying was a labour of love.

There were three dynamos with their engines at Camberwell. The two that have been there since the beginning are small machines; the larger one was new. The smaller machines made a reasonable noise; their straps hummed over the drums, every now and then the brushes buzzed and fizzled, and the air churned steadily, whoo! whoo! whoo! between their poles. One was loose in its foundations and kept the shed vibrating. But the big dynamo drowned these little noises altogether with the sustained drone of its iron core, which somehow set part of the ironwork humming. The place made the visitor's head reel with the throb, throb, throb of the engines, the rotation of the big wheels, the spinning ball-valves, the occasional spittings of the steam, and over all the deep, unceasing, surging note of the big dynamo. This last noise was from an engineering point of view a defect, but Azuma-zi accounted it unto the monster for mightiness and pride.

If it were possible we would have the noises of that shed always about the reader as he reads, we would tell all our story to such an accompaniment. It was a steady stream of din, from which the ear picked out first one thread and then another; there was the intermittent snorting, panting, and seething of the steam engines, the suck and thud of their pistons, the dull beat on the air as the spokes of the great driving wheels came round, a note the leather straps made as they ran tighter and looser, and a fretful tumult from the dynamos; and, over all, sometimes inaudible, as the ear tired of it, and then creeping back upon the senses again, was this trombone note of the big machine. The floor never felt steady and quiet beneath one's feet, but quivered and jarred. It was a confusing, unsteady place, and enough to send anyone's thoughts jerking into odd zigzags. And for three months, while the big strike of the engineers was in progress, Holroyd, who was a blackleg, and Azuma-zi, who was a mere black, were never out of the stir and eddy of it, but slept and fed in the little wooden shanty between the shed and the gates.

Holroyd delivered a theological lecture on the text of his big machine soon after Azuma-zi came. He had to shout to be heard in the din. "Look at that," said Holroyd; "where's your 'eathen idol to match 'im?" And Azuma-zi looked. For a moment Holroyd was inaudible, and then Azuma-zi heard: "Kill a hundred men. Twelve per cent, on the ordinary shares," said Holroyd, "and that's something like a Gord."

Holroyd was proud of his big dynamo, and expatiated upon its size and power to Azuma-zi until heaven knows what odd currents of thought that and the incessant whirling and shindy set up within the curly black cranium. He would explain in the most graphic manner the dozen or so ways in which a man might be killed by it, and once he gave Azuma-zi a shock as a sample of its quality. After that, in the breathing-times of his labour—it was heavy labour, being not only his own, but most of Holroyd's—Azuma-zi would sit and watch the big machine. Now and then the brushes would sparkle and spit blue flashes, at which Holroyd would swear, but all the rest was as smooth and rhythmic as breathing. The band ran shouting over the shaft, and ever behind one as one watched was the complacent thud of the piston. So it lived all day in this big airy shed, with him and Holroyd to wait upon it; not prisoned up and slaving to drive a ship as the other engines he knew—mere captive devils of the British Solomon—had been, but a machine enthroned. Those two smaller dynamos Azuma-zi by force of contrast despised; the large one he privately christened the Lord of the Dynamos. They were fretful and irregular, but the big dynamo was steady. How great it was! How serene and easy in its working! Greater and calmer even than the Buddhas he had seen at Rangoon, and yet not motionless, but living! The great black coils spun, spun, spun, the rings ran round under the brushes, and the deep note of its coil steadied the whole. It affected Azuma-zi queerly.

Azuma-zi was not fond of labour. He would sit about and watch the Lord of the Dynamos while Holroyd went away to persuade the yard porter to get whisky, although his proper place was not in the dynamo shed but behind the engines, and, moreover, if Holroyd caught him skulking he got hit for it with a rod of stout copper wire. He would go and stand close to the colossus, and look up at the great leather band running overhead. There was a black patch on the band that came round, and it pleased him somehow among all the clatter to watch this return again and again. Odd thoughts spun with the whirl of it. Scientific people tell us that savages give souls to rocks and trees,—and a machine is a thousand times more alive than a rock or a tree. And Azuma-zi was practically a savage still; the veneer of civilisation lay no deeper than his slop suit, his bruises, and the coal grime on his face and hands. His father before him had worshipped a meteoric stone, kindred blood, it may be, had splashed the broad wheels of Juggernaut.

He took every opportunity Holroyd gave him of touching and handling the great dynamo that was fascinating him. He polished and cleaned it until the metal parts were blinding in the sun. He felt a mysterious sense of service in doing this. He would go up to it and touch its spinning coils gently. The gods he had worshipped were all far away. The people in London hid their gods.

At last his dim feelings grew more distinct, and took shape in thoughts, and at last in acts. When he came into the roaring shed one morning he salaamed to the Lord of the Dynamos, and then, when Holroyd was away, he went and whispered to the thundering machine that he was its servant, and prayed it to have pity on him and save him from Holroyd. As he did so a rare gleam of light came in through the open archway of the throbbing machine-shed, and the Lord of the Dynamos, as he whirled and roared, was radiant with pale gold. Then Azuma-zi knew that his service was acceptable to his Lord. After that he did not feel so lonely as he had done, and he had indeed been very much alone in London. And even when his work-time was over, which was rare, he loitered about the shed.

Then, the next time Holroyd maltreated him, Azuma-zi went presently to the Lord of the Dynamos and whispered, "Thou seest, O my Lord!" and the angry whirr of the machinery seemed to answer him. Thereafter it appeared to him that whenever Holroyd came into the shed a different note came into the sounds of the dynamo. "My Lord bides his time," said Azuma-zi to himself. "The iniquity of the fool is not yet ripe." And he waited and watched for the day of reckoning. One day there was evidence of short circuiting, and Holroyd, making an unwary examination—it was in the afternoon—got a rather severe shock. Azuma-zi from behind the engine saw him jump off and curse at the peccant coil.

"He is warned," said Azuma-zi to himself. "Surely my Lord is very patient."

Holroyd had at first initiated his "nigger" into such elementary conceptions of the dynamo's working as would enable him to take temporary charge of the shed in his absence. But when he noticed the manner in which Azuma-zi hung about the monster he became suspicious. He dimly perceived his assistant was "up to something," and connecting him with the anointing of the coils with oil that had rotted the varnish in one place, he issued an edict, shouted above the confusion of the machinery, "Don't 'ee go nigh that big dynamo any more, Pooh-bah, or a'll take thy skin off!" Besides, if it pleased Azuma-zi to be near the big machine, it was plain sense and decency to keep him away from it.

Azuma-zi obeyed at the time, but later he was caught bowing before the Lord of the Dynamos. At which Holroyd twisted his arm and kicked him as he turned to go away. As Azuma-zi presently stood behind the engine and glared at the back of the hated Holroyd, the noises of the machinery took a new rhythm, and sounded like four words in his native tongue.

It is hard to say exactly what madness is. I fancy Azuma-zi was mad. The incessant din and whirl of the dynamo shed may have churned up his little store of knowledge and big store of superstitious fancy, at last, into something akin to frenzy. At any rate, when the idea of making Holroyd a sacrifice to the Dynamo Fetich was thus suggested to him, it filled him with a strange tumult of exultant emotion.

That night the two men and their black shadows were alone in the shed together. The shed was lit with one big arc light that winked and flickered purple. The shadows lay black behind the dynamos, the ball governors of the engines whirled from light to darkness, and their pistons beat loud and steady. The world outside seen through the open end of the shed seemed incredibly dim and remote. It seemed absolutely silent, too, since the riot of the machinery drowned every external sound. Far away was the black fence of the yard with grey shadowy houses behind, and above was the deep blue sky and the pale little stars. Azuma-zi suddenly walked across the centre of the shed above which the leather bands were running, and went into the shadow by the big dynamo. Holroyd heard a click, and the spin of the armature changed.

"What are you dewin' with that switch?" he bawled in surprise. "Han't I told you——"

Then he saw the set expression of Azuma-zi's eyes as the Asiatic came out of the shadow towards him.

In another moment the two men were grappling fiercely in front of the great dynamo.

"You coffee-headed fool!" gasped Holroyd, with a brown hand at his throat. "Keep off those contact rings." In another moment he was tripped and reeling back upon the Lord of the Dynamos. He instinctively loosened his grip upon his antagonist to save himself from the machine.

The messenger, sent in furious haste from the station to find out what had happened in the dynamo shed, met Azuma-zi at the porter's lodge by the gate. Azuma-zi tried to explain something, but the messenger could make nothing of the black's incoherent English, and hurried on to the shed. The machines were all noisily at work, and nothing seemed to be disarranged. There was, however, a queer smell of singed hair. Then he saw an odd-looking crumpled mass clinging to the front of the big dynamo, and, approaching, recognised the distorted remains of Holroyd.

The man stared and hesitated a moment. Then he saw the face, and shut his eyes convulsively. He turned on his heel before he opened them, so that he should not see Holroyd again, and went out of the shed to get advice and help.

When Azuma-zi saw Holroyd die in the grip of the Great Dynamo he had been a little scared about the consequences of his act. Yet he felt strangely elated, and knew that the favour of the Lord Dynamo was upon him. His plan was already settled when he met the man coming from the station, and the scientific manager who speedily arrived on the scene jumped at the obvious conclusion of suicide. This expert scarcely noticed Azuma-zi, except to ask a few questions. Did he see Holroyd kill himself? Azuma-zi explained he had been out of sight at the engine furnace until he heard a difference in the noise from the dynamo. It was not a difficult examination, being untinctured by suspicion.

The distorted remains of Holroyd, which the electrician removed from the machine, were hastily covered by the porter with a coffee-stained table-cloth. Somebody, by a happy inspiration, fetched a medical man. The expert was chiefly anxious to get the machine at work again, for seven or eight trains had stopped midway in the stuffy tunnels of the electric railway. Azuma-zi, answering or misunderstanding the questions of the people who had by authority or impudence come into the shed, was presently sent back to the stoke-hole by the scientific manager. Of course a crowd collected outside the gates of the yard—a crowd, for no known reason, always hovers for a day or two near the scene of a sudden death in London—two or three reporters percolated somehow into the engine-shed, and one even got to Azuma-zi; but the scientific expert cleared them out again, being himself an amateur journalist.

Presently the body was carried away, and public interest departed with it. Azuma-zi remained very quietly at his furnace, seeing over and over again in the coals a figure that wriggled violently and became still. An hour after the murder, to any one coming into the shed it would have looked exactly as if nothing remarkable had ever happened there. Peeping presently from his engine-room the black saw the Lord Dynamo spin and whirl beside his little brothers, and the driving wheels were beating round, and the steam in the pistons went thud, thud, exactly as it had been earlier in the evening. After all, from the mechanical point of view, it had been a most insignificant incident—the mere temporary deflection of a current. But now the slender form and slender shadow of the scientific manager replaced the sturdy outline of Holroyd travelling up and down the lane of light upon the vibrating floor under the straps between the engines and the dynamos.

"Have I not served my Lord?" said Azuma-zi inaudibly, from his shadow, and the note of the great dynamo rang out full and clear. As he looked at the big whirling mechanism the strange fascination of it that had been a little in abeyance since Holroyd's death resumed its sway.

Never had Azuma-zi seen a man killed so swiftly and pitilessly. The big humming machine had slain its victim without wavering for a second from its steady beating. It was indeed a mighty god.

The unconscious scientific manager stood with his back to him, scribbling on a piece of paper. His shadow lay at the foot of the monster.

Was the Lord Dynamo still hungry? His servant was ready.

Azuma-zi made a stealthy step forward; then stopped. The scientific manager suddenly ceased his writing, walked down the shed to the endmost of the dynamos, and began to examine the brushes.

Azuma-zi hesitated, and then slipped across noiselessly into the shadow by the switch. There he waited. Presently the manager's footsteps could be heard returning. He stopped in his old position, unconscious of the stoker crouching ten feet away from him. Then the big dynamo suddenly fizzled, and in another moment Azuma-zi had sprung out of the darkness upon him.

First, the scientific manager was gripped round the body and swung towards the big dynamo, then, kicking with his knee and forcing his antagonist's head down with his hands, he loosened the grip on his waist and swung round away from the machine. Then the black grasped him again, putting a curly head against his chest, and they swayed and panted as it seemed for an age or so. Then the scientific manager was impelled to catch a black ear in his teeth and bite furiously. The black yelled hideously.

They rolled over on the floor, and the black, who had apparently slipped from the vice of the teeth or parted with some ear—the scientific manager wondered which at the time—tried to throttle him. The scientific manager was making some ineffectual efforts to claw something with his hands and to kick, when the welcome sound of quick footsteps sounded on the floor. The next moment Azuma-zi had left him and darted towards the big dynamo. There was a splutter amid the roar.

The officer of the company who had entered stood staring as Azuma-zi caught the naked terminals in his hands, gave one horrible convulsion, and then hung motionless from the machine, his face violently distorted.

"I'm jolly glad you came in when you did," said the scientific manager, still sitting on the floor.

He looked at the still quivering figure. "It is not a nice death to die, apparently—but it is quick."

The official was still staring at the body. He was a man of slow apprehension.

There was a pause.

The scientific manager got up on his feet rather awkwardly. He ran his fingers along his collar thoughtfully, and moved his head to and fro several times.

"Poor Holroyd! I see now." Then almost mechanically he went towards the switch in the shadow and turned the current into the railway circuit again. As he did so the singed body loosened its grip upon the machine and fell forward on its face. The core of the dynamo roared out loud and clear, and the armature beat the air.

So ended prematurely the worship of the Dynamo Deity, perhaps the most short-lived of all religions. Yet withal it could at least boast a Martyrdom and a Human Sacrifice.

IX.

THE MOTH.

Probably you have heard of Hapley—not W. T. Hapley, the son, but the celebrated Hapley, the Hapley of Periplaneta Hapliia, Hapley the entomologist.

If so you know at least of the great feud between Hapley and Professor Pawkins, though certain of its consequences may be new to you. For those who have not, a word or two of explanation is necessary, which the idle reader may go over with a glancing eye, if his indolence so incline him.

It is amazing how very widely diffused is the ignorance of such really important matters as this Hapley-Pawkins feud. Those epoch-making controversies, again, that have convulsed the Geological Society are, I verily believe, almost entirely unknown outside the fellowship of that body. I have heard men of fair general education even refer to the great scenes at these meetings as vestry-meeting squabbles. Yet the great hate of the English and Scotch geologists has lasted now half a century, and has "left deep and abundant marks upon the body of the science." And this Hapley-Pawkins business, though perhaps a more personal affair, stirred passions as profound, if not profounder. Your common man has no conception of the zeal that animates a scientific investigator, the fury of contradiction you can arouse in him. It is the odium theologicum in a new form. There are men, for instance, who would gladly burn Professor Ray Lankester at Smithfield for his treatment of the Mollusca in the Encyclopaedia. That fantastic extension of the Cephalopods to cover the Pteropods ... But I wander from Hapley and Pawkins.

It began years and years ago, with a revision of the Microlepidoptera (whatever these may be) by Pawkins, in which he extinguished a new species created by Hapley. Hapley, who was always quarrelsome, replied by a stinging impeachment of the entire classification of Pawkins.[A] Pawkins in his "Rejoinder"[B] suggested that Hapley's microscope was as defective as his power of observation, and called him an "irresponsible meddler"— Hapley was not a professor at that time. Hapley in his retort,[C] spoke of "blundering collectors," and described, as if inadvertently, Pawkins' revision as a "miracle of ineptitude." It was war to the knife. However, it would scarcely interest the reader to detail how these two great men quarrelled, and how the split between them widened until from the Microlepidoptera they were at war upon every open question in entomology. There were memorable occasions. At times the Royal Entomological Society meetings resembled nothing so much as the Chamber of Deputies. On the whole, I fancy Pawkins was nearer the truth than Hapley. But Hapley was skilful with his rhetoric, had a turn for ridicule rare in a scientific man, was endowed with vast energy, and had a fine sense of injury in the matter of the extinguished species; while Pawkins was a man of dull presence, prosy of speech, in shape not unlike a water-barrel, over conscientious with testimonials, and suspected of jobbing museum appointments. So the young men gathered round Hapley and applauded him. It was a long struggle, vicious from the beginning and growing at last to pitiless antagonism. The successive turns of fortune, now an advantage to one side and now to another—now Hapley tormented by some success of Pawkins, and now Pawkins outshone by Hapley, belong rather to the history of entomology than to this story.

[Footnote A: "Remarks on a Recent Revision of Microlepidoptera." Quart. Journ. Entomological Soc., 1863.]

[Footnote B: "Rejoinder to certain Remarks," etc. Ibid. 1864.]

[Footnote C: "Further Remarks," etc. Ibid.]

But in 1891 Pawkins, whose health had been bad for some time, published some work upon the "mesoblast" of the Death's Head Moth. What the mesoblast of the Death's Head Moth may be does not matter a rap in this story. But the work was far below his usual standard, and gave Hapley an opening he had coveted for years. He must have worked night and day to make the most of his advantage.

In an elaborate critique he rent Pawkins to tatters—one can fancy the man's disordered black hair, and his queer dark eyes flashing as he went for his antagonist—and Pawkins made a reply, halting, ineffectual, with painful gaps of silence, and yet malignant. There was no mistaking his will to wound Hapley, nor his incapacity to do it. But few of those who heard him—I was absent from that meeting—realised how ill the man was.

Hapley got his opponent down, and meant to finish him. He followed with a simply brutal attack upon Pawkins, in the form of a paper upon the development of moths in general, a paper showing evidence of a most extraordinary amount of mental labour, and yet couched in a violently controversial tone. Violent as it was, an editorial note witnesses that it was modified. It must have covered Pawkins with shame and confusion of face. It left no loophole; it was murderous in argument, and utterly contemptuous in tone; an awful thing for the declining years of a man's career.

The world of entomologists waited breathlessly for the rejoinder from Pawkins. He would try one, for Pawkins had always been game. But when it came it surprised them. For the rejoinder of Pawkins was to catch influenza, proceed to pneumonia, and die.

It was perhaps as effectual a reply as he could make under the circumstances, and largely turned the current of feeling against Hapley. The very people who had most gleefully cheered on those gladiators became serious at the consequence. There could be no reasonable doubt the fret of the defeat had contributed to the death of Pawkins. There was a limit even to scientific controversy, said serious people. Another crushing attack was already in the press and appeared on the day before the funeral. I don't think Hapley exerted himself to stop it. People remembered how Hapley had hounded down his rival, and forgot that rival's defects. Scathing satire reads ill over fresh mould. The thing provoked comment in the daily papers. This it was that made me think that you had probably heard of Hapley and this controversy. But, as I have already remarked, scientific workers live very much in a world of their own; half the people, I dare say, who go along Piccadilly to the Academy every year, could not tell you where the learned societies abide. Many even think that research is a kind of happy-family cage in which all kinds of men lie down together in peace.

In his private thoughts Hapley could not forgive Pawkins for dying. In the first place, it was a mean dodge to escape the absolute pulverisation Hapley had in hand for him, and in the second, it left Hapley's mind with a queer gap in it. For twenty years he had worked hard, sometimes far into the night, and seven days a week, with microscope, scalpel, collecting-net, and pen, and almost entirely with reference to Pawkins. The European reputation he had won had come as an incident in that great antipathy. He had gradually worked up to a climax in this last controversy. It had killed Pawkins, but it had also thrown Hapley out of gear, so to speak, and his doctor advised him to give up work for a time, and rest. So Hapley went down into a quiet village in Kent, and thought day and night of Pawkins, and good things it was now impossible to say about him.

At last Hapley began to realise in what direction the pre-occupation tended. He determined to make a fight for it, and started by trying to read novels. But he could not get his mind off Pawkins, white in the face and making his last speech—every sentence a beautiful opening for Hapley. He turned to fiction—and found it had no grip on him. He read the "Island Nights' Entertainments" until his "sense of causation" was shocked beyond endurance by the Bottle Imp. Then he went to Kipling, and found he "proved nothing," besides being irreverent and vulgar. These scientific people have their limitations. Then unhappily, he tried Besant's "Inner House," and the opening chapter set his mind upon learned societies and Pawkins at once.

So Hapley turned to chess, and found it a little more soothing. He soon mastered the moves and the chief gambits and commoner closing positions, and began to beat the Vicar. But then the cylindrical contours of the opposite king began to resemble Pawkins standing up and gasping ineffectually against check-mate, and Hapley decided to give up chess.

Perhaps the study of some new branch of science would after all be better diversion. The best rest is change of occupation. Hapley determined to plunge at diatoms, and had one of his smaller microscopes and Halibut's monograph sent down from London. He thought that perhaps if he could get up a vigorous quarrel with Halibut, he might be able to begin life afresh and forget Pawkins. And very soon he was hard at work in his habitual strenuous fashion, at these microscopic denizens of the way-side pool.

It was on the third day of the diatoms that Hapley became aware of a novel addition to the local fauna. He was working late at the microscope, and the only light in the room was the brilliant little lamp with the special form of green shade. Like all experienced microscopists, he kept both eyes open. It is the only way to avoid excessive fatigue. One eye was over the instrument, and bright and distinct before that was the circular field of the microscope, across which a brown diatom was slowly moving. With the other eye Hapley saw, as it were, without seeing. He was only dimly conscious of the brass side of the instrument, the illuminated part of the table-cloth, a sheet of notepaper, the foot of the lamp, and the darkened room beyond.

Suddenly his attention drifted from one eye to the other. The table-cloth was of the material called tapestry by shopmen, and rather brightly coloured. The pattern was in gold, with a small amount of crimson and pale blue upon a greyish ground. At one point the pattern seemed displaced, and there was a vibrating movement of the colours at this point.

Hapley suddenly moved his head back and looked with both eyes. His mouth fell open with astonishment.

It was a large moth or butterfly; its wings spread in butterfly fashion!

It was strange it should be in the room at all, for the windows were closed. Strange that it should not have attracted his attention when fluttering to its present position. Strange that it should match the table-cloth. Stranger far that to him, Hapley, the great entomologist, it was altogether unknown. There was no delusion. It was crawling slowly towards the foot of the lamp.

"New Genus, by heavens! And in England!" said Hapley, staring.

Then he suddenly thought of Pawkins. Nothing would have maddened Pawkins more...And Pawkins was dead!

Something about the head and body of the insect became singularly suggestive of Pawkins, just as the chess king had been.

"Confound Pawkins!" said Hapley. "But I must catch this." And looking round him for some means of capturing the moth, he rose slowly out of his chair. Suddenly the insect rose, struck the edge of the lampshade—Hapley heard the "ping"—and vanished into the shadow.

In a moment Hapley had whipped off the shade, so that the whole room was illuminated. The thing had disappeared, but soon his practised eye detected it upon the wall-paper near the door. He went towards it poising the lamp-shade for capture. Before he was within striking distance, however, it had risen and was fluttering round the room. After the fashion of its kind, it flew with sudden starts and turns, seeming to vanish here and reappear there. Once Hapley struck, and missed; then again.

The third time he hit his microscope. The instrument swayed, struck and overturned the lamp, and fell noisily upon the floor. The lamp turned over on the table and, very luckily, went out. Hapley was left in the dark. With a start he felt the strange moth blunder into his face.

It was maddening. He had no lights. If he opened the door of the room the thing would get away. In the darkness he saw Pawkins quite distinctly laughing at him. Pawkins had ever an oily laugh. He swore furiously and stamped his foot on the floor.

There was a timid rapping at the door.

Then it opened, perhaps a foot, and very slowly. The alarmed face of the landlady appeared behind a pink candle flame; she wore a night-cap over her grey hair and had some purple garment over her shoulders. "What was that fearful smash?" she said. "Has anything——" The strange moth appeared fluttering about the chink of the door. "Shut that door!" said Hapley, and suddenly rushed at her.

The door slammed hastily. Hapley was left alone in the dark. Then in the pause he heard his landlady scuttle upstairs, lock her door, and drag something heavy across the room and put against it.

It became evident to Hapley that his conduct and appearance had been strange and alarming. Confound the moth! and

Pawkins! However, it was a pity to lose the moth now. He felt his way into the hall and found the matches, after sending his hat down upon the floor with a noise like a drum. With the lighted candle he returned to the sitting-room. No moth was to be seen. Yet once for a moment it seemed that the thing was fluttering round his head. Hapley very suddenly decided to give up the moth and go to bed. But he was excited. All night long his sleep was broken by dreams of the moth, Pawkins, and his landlady. Twice in the night he turned out and soused his head in cold water.

One thing was very clear to him. His landlady could not possibly understand about the strange moth, especially as he had failed to catch it. No one but an entomologist would understand quite how he felt. She was probably frightened at his behaviour, and yet he failed to see how he could explain it. He decided to say nothing further about the events of last night. After breakfast he saw her in her garden, and decided to go out and talk to reassure her. He talked to her about beans and potatoes, bees, caterpillars, and the price of fruit. She replied in her usual manner, but she looked at him a little suspiciously, and kept walking as he walked, so that there was always a bed of flowers, or a row of beans, or something of the sort, between them. After a while he began to feel singularly irritated at this, and to conceal his vexation went indoors and presently went out for a walk.

The moth, or butterfly, trailing an odd flavour of Pawkins with it, kept coming into that walk, though he did his best to keep his mind off it. Once he saw it quite distinctly, with its wings flattened out, upon the old stone wall that runs along the west edge of the park, but going up to it he found it was only two lumps of grey and yellow lichen. "This," said Hapley, "is the reverse of mimicry. Instead of a butterfly looking like a stone, here is a stone looking like a butterfly!" Once something hovered and fluttered round his head, but by an effort of will he drove that impression out of his mind again.

In the afternoon Hapley called upon the Vicar, and argued with him upon theological questions. They sat in the little arbour covered with briar, and smoked as they wrangled. "Look at that moth!" said Hapley, suddenly, pointing to the edge of the wooden table.

"Where?" said the Vicar.

"You don't see a moth on the edge of the table there?" said Hapley.

"Certainly not," said the Vicar.

Hapley was thunderstruck. He gasped. The Vicar was staring at him. Clearly the man saw nothing. "The eye of faith is no better than the eye of science," said Hapley awkwardly.

"I don't see your point," said the Vicar, thinking it was part of the argument.

That night Hapley found the moth crawling over his counterpane. He sat on the edge of the bed in his shirt sleeves and reasoned with himself. Was it pure hallucination? He knew he was slipping, and he battled for his sanity with the same silent energy he had formerly displayed against Pawkins. So persistent is mental habit, that he felt as if it were still a struggle with Pawkins. He was well versed in psychology. He knew that such visual illusions do come as a result of mental strain. But the point was, he did not only see the moth, he had heard it when it touched the edge of the lampshade, and afterwards when it hit against the wall, and he had felt it strike his face in the dark.

He looked at it. It was not at all dreamlike, but perfectly clear and solid-looking in the candle-light. He saw the hairy body, and the short feathery antennae, the jointed legs, even a place where the down was rubbed from the wing. He suddenly felt angry with himself for being afraid of a little insect.

His landlady had got the servant to sleep with her that night, because she was afraid to be alone. In addition she had locked the door, and put the chest of drawers against it. They listened and talked in whispers after they had gone to bed, but nothing occurred to alarm them. About eleven they had ventured to put the candle out, and had both dozed off to sleep. They woke up with a start, and sat up in bed, listening in the darkness.

Then they heard slippered feet going to and fro in Hapley's room. A chair was overturned, and there was a violent dab at the wall. Then a china mantel ornament smashed upon the fender. Suddenly the door of the room opened, and they heard him upon the landing. They clung to one another, listening. He seemed to be dancing upon the staircase. Now he would go down three or four steps quickly, then up again, then hurry down into the hall. They heard the umbrella stand go over, and the fanlight break. Then the bolt shot and the chain rattled. He was opening the door.

They hurried to the window. It was a dim grey night; an almost unbroken sheet of watery cloud was sweeping across the moon, and the hedge and trees in front of the house were black against the pale roadway. They saw Hapley, looking like a ghost in his shirt and white trousers, running to and fro in the road, and beating the air. Now he would stop, now he would dart very rapidly at something invisible, now he would move upon it with stealthy strides. At last he went out of sight up the road towards the down. Then, while they argued who should go down and lock the door, he returned. He was walking very fast, and he came straight into the house, closed the door carefully, and went quietly up to his bedroom. Then everything was silent.

"Mrs. Colville," said Hapley, calling down the staircase next morning, "I hope I did not alarm you last night."

"You may well ask that!" said Mrs. Colville.

"The fact is, I am a sleep-walker, and the last two nights I have been without my sleeping mixture. There is nothing to be alarmed about, really. I am sorry I made such an ass of myself. I will go over the down to Shoreham, and get some stuff to make me sleep soundly. I ought to have done that yesterday."

But half-way over the down, by the chalk pits, the moth came upon Hapley again. He went on, trying to keep his mind upon chess problems, but it was no good. The thing fluttered into his face, and he struck at it with his hat in self-defence. Then rage, the old rage—the rage he had so often felt against Pawkins—came upon him again. He went on, leaping and striking at the eddying insect. Suddenly he trod on nothing, and fell headlong.

There was a gap in his sensations, and Hapley found himself sitting on the heap of flints in front of the opening of the chalk-pits, with a leg twisted back under him. The strange moth was still fluttering round his head. He struck at it with his hand, and turning his head saw two men approaching him. One was the village doctor. It occurred to Hapley that this was lucky. Then it came into his mind with extraordinary vividness, that no one would ever be able to see the strange moth except himself, and that it behoved him to keep silent about it.

Late that night, however, after his broken leg was set, he was feverish and forgot his self-restraint. He was lying flat on his bed, and he began to run his eyes round the room to see if the moth was still about. He tried not to do this, but it was no good. He soon caught sight of the thing resting close to his hand, by the night-light, on the green table-cloth. The wings quivered. With a sudden wave of anger he smote at it with his fist, and the nurse woke up with a shriek. He had missed it.

"That moth!" he said; and then, "It was fancy. Nothing!"

All the time he could see quite clearly the insect going round the cornice and darting across the room, and he could also see that the nurse saw nothing of it and looked at him strangely. He must keep himself in hand. He knew he was a lost man if he did not keep himself in hand. But as the night waned the fever grew upon him, and the very dread he had of seeing the moth made him see it. About five, just as the dawn was grey, he tried to get out of bed and catch it, though his leg was afire with pain. The nurse had to struggle with him.

On account of this, they tied him down to the bed. At this the moth grew bolder, and once he felt it settle in his hair. Then, because he struck out violently with his arms, they tied these also. At this the moth came and crawled over his face, and Hapley wept, swore, screamed, prayed for them to take it off him, unavailingly.

The doctor was a blockhead, a just-qualified general practitioner, and quite ignorant of mental science. He simply said there was no moth. Had he possessed the wit, he might still, perhaps, have saved Hapley from his fate by entering into his delusion, and covering his face with gauze, as he prayed might be done. But, as I say, the doctor was a blockhead, and until the leg was healed Hapley was kept tied to his bed, and with the imaginary moth crawling over him. It never left him while he was awake and it grew to a monster in his dreams. While he was awake he longed for sleep, and from sleep he awoke screaming.

So now Hapley is spending the remainder of his days in a padded room, worried by a moth that no one else can see. The asylum doctor calls it hallucination; but Hapley, when he is in his easier mood, and can talk, says it is the ghost of Pawkins, and consequently a unique specimen and well worth the trouble of catching.

X.

THE TREASURE IN THE FOREST.

The canoe was now approaching the land. The bay opened out, and a gap in the white surf of the reef marked where the little river ran out to the sea; the thicker and deeper green of the virgin forest showed its course down the distant hill slope. The forest here came close to the beach. Far beyond, dim and almost cloudlike in texture, rose the mountains, like suddenly frozen waves. The sea was still save for an almost imperceptible swell. The sky blazed.

The man with the carved paddle stopped. "It should be somewhere here," he said. He shipped the paddle and held his arms out straight before him.

The other man had been in the fore part of the canoe, closely scrutinising the land. He had a sheet of yellow paper on his knee.

"Come and look at this, Evans," he said.

Both men spoke in low tones, and their lips were hard and dry.

The man called Evans came swaying along the canoe until he could look over his companion's shoulder.

The paper had the appearance of a rough map. By much folding it was creased and worn to the pitch of separation, and the second man held the discoloured fragments together where they had parted. On it one could dimly make out, in almost obliterated pencil, the outline of the bay.

"Here," said Evans, "is the reef, and here is the gap." He ran his thumb-nail over the chart.

"This curved and twisting line is the river—I could do with a drink now!—and this star is the place."

"You see this dotted line," said the man with the map; "it is a straight line, and runs from the opening of the reef to a clump of palm-trees. The star comes just where it cuts the river. We must mark the place as we go into the lagoon."

"It's queer," said Evans, after a pause, "what these little marks down here are for. It looks like the plan of a house or something; but what all these little dashes, pointing this way and that, may mean I can't get a notion. And what's the writing?"

"Chinese," said the man with the map.

"Of course! He was a Chinee," said Evans.

"They all were," said the man with the map.

They both sat for some minutes staring at the land, while the canoe drifted slowly. Then Evans looked towards the paddle.

"Your turn with the paddle now, Hooker," said he.

And his companion quietly folded up his map, put it in his pocket, passed Evans carefully, and began to paddle. His movements were languid, like those of a man whose strength was nearly exhausted.

Evans sat with his eyes half closed, watching the frothy breakwater of the coral creep nearer and nearer. The sky was like a furnace, for the sun was near the zenith. Though they were so near the Treasure he did not feel the exaltation he had anticipated. The intense excitement of the struggle for the plan, and the long night voyage from the mainland in the unprovisioned canoe had, to use his own expression, "taken it out of him." He tried to arouse himself by directing his mind to the ingots the Chinamen had spoken of, but it would not rest there; it came back headlong to the thought of sweet water rippling in the river, and to the almost unendurable dryness of his lips and throat. The rhythmic wash of the sea upon the reef was becoming audible now, and it had a pleasant sound in his ears; the water washed along the side of the canoe, and the paddle dripped between each stroke. Presently he began to doze.

He was still dimly conscious of the island, but a queer dream texture interwove with his sensations. Once again it was the night when he and Hooker had hit upon the Chinamen's secret; he saw the moonlit trees, the little fire burning, and the black figures of the three Chinamen—silvered on one side by moonlight, and on the other glowing from the firelight—and heard them talking together in pigeon-English—for they came from different provinces. Hooker had caught the drift of their talk first, and had motioned to him to listen. Fragments of the conversation were inaudible, and fragments incomprehensible. A Spanish galleon from the Philippines hopelessly aground, and its treasure buried against the day of return, lay in the background of the story; a shipwrecked crew thinned by disease, a quarrel or so, and the needs of discipline, and at last taking to their boats never to be heard of again. Then Chang-hi, only a year since, wandering ashore, had happened upon the ingots hidden for two hundred years, had deserted his junk, and reburied them with infinite toil, single-handed but very safe. He laid great stress on the safety—it was a secret of his. Now he wanted help to return and exhume them. Presently the little map fluttered and the voices sank. A fine story for two, stranded British wastrels to hear! Evans' dream shifted to the moment when he had Chang-hi's pigtail in his hand. The life of a Chinaman is scarcely sacred like a European's. The cunning little face of Chang-hi, first keen and furious like a startled snake, and then fearful, treacherous, and pitiful, became overwhelmingly prominent in the dream. At the end Chang-hi had grinned, a most incomprehensible and startling grin. Abruptly things became very unpleasant, as they will do at times in dreams. Chang-hi gibbered and threatened him. He saw in his dream heaps and heaps of gold, and Chang-hi intervening and struggling to hold him back from it. He took Chang-hi by the pig-tail—how big the yellow brute was, and how he struggled and grinned! He kept growing bigger, too. Then the bright heaps of gold turned to a roaring furnace, and a vast devil, surprisingly like Chang-hi, but with a huge black tail, began to feed him with coals. They burnt his mouth horribly. Another devil was shouting his name: "Evans, Evans, you sleepy fool!"—or was it Hooker?

He woke up. They were in the mouth of the lagoon.

"There are the three palm-trees. It must be in a line with that clump of bushes," said his companion. "Mark that. If we, go to those bushes and then strike into the bush in a straight line from here, we shall come to it when we come to the stream."

They could see now where the mouth of the stream opened out. At the sight of it Evans revived. "Hurry up, man," he said, "or by heaven I shall have to drink sea water!" He gnawed his hand and stared at the gleam of silver among the rocks and green tangle.

Presently he turned almost fiercely upon Hooker. "Give me the paddle," he said.

So they reached the river mouth. A little way up Hooker took some water in the hollow of his hand, tasted it, and spat it out. A little further he tried again. "This will do," he said, and they began drinking eagerly.

"Curse this!" said Evans suddenly. "It's too slow." And, leaning dangerously over the fore part of the canoe, he began to suck up the water with his lips.

Presently they made an end of drinking, and, running the canoe into a little creek, were about to land among the thick growth that overhung the water.

"We shall have to scramble through this to the beach to find our bushes and get the line to the place," said Evans.

"We had better paddle round," said Hooker.

So they pushed out again into the river and paddled back down it to the sea, and along the shore to the place where the clump of bushes grew. Here they landed, pulled the light canoe far up the beach, and then went up towards the edge of the jungle until they could see the opening of the reef and the bushes in a straight line. Evans had taken a native implement out of the canoe. It was L-shaped, and the transverse piece was armed with polished stone. Hooker carried the paddle. "It is straight now in this direction," said he; "we must push through this till we strike the stream. Then we must prospect."

They pushed through a close tangle of reeds, broad fronds, and young trees, and at first it was toilsome going, but very speedily the trees became larger and the ground beneath them opened out. The blaze of the sunlight was replaced by insensible degrees by cool shadow. The trees became at last vast pillars that rose up to a canopy of greenery far overhead. Dim white flowers hung from their stems, and ropy creepers swung from tree to tree. The shadow deepened. On the ground, blotched fungi and a red-brown incrustation became frequent.

Evans shivered. "It seems almost cold here after the blaze outside."

"I hope we are keeping to the straight," said Hooker.

Presently they saw, far ahead, a gap in the sombre darkness where white shafts of hot sunlight smote into the forest. There also was brilliant green undergrowth and coloured flowers. Then they heard the rush of water.

"Here is the river. We should be close to it now," said Hooker.

The vegetation was thick by the river bank. Great plants, as yet unnamed, grew among the roots of the big trees, and spread rosettes of huge green fans towards the strip of sky. Many flowers and a creeper with shiny foliage clung to the exposed stems. On the water of the broad, quiet pool which the treasure-seekers now overlooked there floated big oval leaves and a waxen, pinkish-white flower not unlike a water-lily. Further, as the river bent away from them, the water suddenly frothed and became noisy in a rapid.

"Well?" said Evans.

"We have swerved a little from the straight," said Hooker. "That was to be expected."

He turned and looked into the dim cool shadows of the silent forest behind them. "If we beat a little way up and down the stream we should come to something."

"You said—" began Evans.

"He said there was a heap of stones," said Hooker.

The two men looked at each other for a moment.

"Let us try a little down-stream first," said Evans.

They advanced slowly, looking curiously about them. Suddenly Evans stopped. "What the devil's that?" he said.

Hooker followed his finger. "Something blue," he said. It had come into view as they topped a gentle swell of the ground. Then he began to distinguish what it was.

He advanced suddenly with hasty steps, until the body that belonged to the limp hand and arm had become visible. His grip tightened on the implement he carried. The thing was the figure of a Chinaman lying on his face. The abandon of the pose was unmistakable.

The two men drew closer together, and stood staring silently at this ominous dead body. It lay in a clear space among the trees. Near by was a spade after the Chinese pattern, and further off lay a scattered heap of stones, close to a freshly dug hole.

"Somebody has been here before," said Hooker, clearing his throat.

Then suddenly Evans began to swear and rave, and stamp upon the ground.

Hooker turned white but said nothing. He advanced towards the prostrate body. He saw the neck was puffed and purple, and the hands and ankles swollen. "Pah!" he said, and suddenly turned away and went towards the excavation. He gave a cry of surprise. He shouted to Evans, who was following him slowly.

"You fool! It's all right. It's here still." Then he turned again and looked at the dead Chinaman, and then again at the hole.

Evans hurried to the hole. Already half exposed by the ill-fated wretch beside them lay a number of dull yellow bars. He bent down in the hole, and, clearing off the soil with his bare hands, hastily pulled one of the heavy masses out. As he did so a little thorn pricked his hand. He pulled the delicate spike out with his fingers and lifted the ingot.

"Only gold or lead could weigh like this," he said exultantly.

Hooker was still looking at the dead Chinaman. He was puzzled.

"He stole a march on his friends," he said at last. "He came here alone, and some poisonous snake has killed him... I wonder how he found the place."

Evans stood with the ingot in his hands. What did a dead Chinaman signify? "We shall have to take this stuff to the mainland piecemeal, and bury it there for a while. How shall we get it to the canoe?"

He took his jacket off and spread it on the ground, and flung two or three ingots into it. Presently he found that another little thorn had punctured his skin.

"This is as much as we can carry," said he. Then suddenly, with a queer rush of irritation, "What are you staring at?"

Hooker turned to him. "I can't stand him ..." He nodded towards the corpse. "It's so like——"

"Rubbish!" said Evans. "All Chinamen are alike."

Hooker looked into his face. "I'm going to bury that, anyhow, before I lend a hand with this stuff."

"Don't be a fool, Hooker," said Evans, "Let that mass of corruption bide."

Hooker hesitated, and then his eye went carefully over the brown soil about them. "It scares me somehow," he said.

"The thing is," said Evans, "what to do with these ingots. Shall we re-bury them over here, or take them across the strait in the canoe?"

Hooker thought. His puzzled gaze wandered among the tall tree-trunks, and up into the remote sunlit greenery overhead. He shivered again as his eye rested upon the blue figure of the

Chinaman. He stared searchingly among the grey depths between the trees.

"What's come to you, Hooker?" said Evans. "Have you lost your wits?"

"Let's get the gold out of this place, anyhow," said Hooker.

He took the ends of the collar of the coat in his hands, and Evans took the opposite corners, and they lifted the mass. "Which way?" said Evans. "To the canoe?"

"It's queer," said Evans, when they had advanced only a few steps, "but my arms ache still with that paddling."

"Curse it!" he said. "But they ache! I must rest."

They let the coat down, Evans' face was white, and little drops of sweat stood out upon his forehead. "It's stuffy, somehow, in this forest."

Then with an abrupt transition to unreasonable anger: "What is the good of waiting here all the day? Lend a hand, I say! You have done nothing but moon since we saw the dead Chinaman."

Hooker was looking steadfastly at his companion's face. He helped raise the coat bearing the ingots, and they went forward perhaps a hundred yards in silence. Evans began to breathe heavily. "Can't you speak?" he said.

"What's the matter with you?" said Hooker.

Evans stumbled, and then with a sudden curse flung the coat from him. He stood for a moment staring at Hooker, and then with a groan clutched at his own throat.

"Don't come near me," he said, and went and leant against a tree. Then in a steadier voice, "I'll be better in a minute."

Presently his grip upon the trunk loosened, and he slipped slowly down the stem of the tree until he was a crumpled heap at its foot. His hands were clenched convulsively. His face became distorted with pain. Hooker approached him.

"Don't touch me! Don't touch me!" said Evans in a stifled voice. "Put the gold back on the coat."

"Can't I do anything for you?" said Hooker.

"Put the gold back on the coat."

As Hooker handled the ingots he felt a little prick on the ball of his thumb. He looked at his hand and saw a slender thorn, perhaps two inches in length.

Evans gave an inarticulate cry and rolled over.

Hooker's jaw dropped. He stared at the thorn for a moment with dilated eyes. Then he looked at Evans, who was now crumpled together on the ground, his back bending and straightening spasmodically. Then he looked through the pillars of the trees and net-work of creeper stems, to where in the dim grey shadow the blue-clad body of the Chinaman was still indistinctly visible. He thought of the little dashes in the corner of the plan, and in a moment he understood.

"God help me!" he said. For the thorns were similar to those the Dyaks poison and use in their blowing-tubes. He understood now what Chang-hi's assurance of the safety of his treasure meant. He understood that grin now.

"Evans!" he cried.

But Evans was silent and motionless, save for a horrible spasmodic twitching of his limbs. A profound silence brooded over the forest.

Then Hooker began to suck furiously at the little pink spot on the ball of his thumb—sucking for dear life. Presently he felt a strange aching pain in his arms and shoulders, and his fingers seemed difficult to bend. Then he knew that sucking was no good.

Abruptly he stopped, and sitting down by the pile of ingots, and resting his chin upon his hands and his elbows upon his knees, stared at the distorted but still quivering body of his companion. Chang-hi's grin came into his mind again. The dull pain spread towards his throat and grew slowly in intensity. Far above him a faint breeze stirred the greenery, and the white petals of some unknown flower came floating down through the gloom.

XI.

THE STORY OF THE LATE MR. ELVESHAM.

I set this story down, not expecting it will be believed, but, if possible, to prepare a way of escape for the next victim. He, perhaps, may profit by my misfortune. My own case, I know, is hopeless, and I am now in some measure prepared to meet my fate.

My name is Edward George Eden. I was born at Trentham, in Staffordshire, my father being employed in the gardens there. I lost my mother when I was three years old, and my father when I was five, my uncle, George Eden, then adopting me as his own son. He was a single man, self-educated, and well-known in Birmingham as an enterprising journalist; he educated me generously, fired my ambition to succeed in the world, and at his death, which happened four years ago, left me his entire fortune, a matter of about five hundred pounds after all outgoing charges were paid. I was then eighteen. He advised me in his will to expend the money in completing my education. I had already chosen the profession of medicine, and through his posthumous generosity and my good fortune in a scholarship competition, I became a medical student at University College, London. At the time of the beginning of my story I lodged at 11A University Street in a little upper room, very shabbily furnished and draughty, overlooking the back of Shoolbred's premises. I used this little room both to live in and sleep in, because I was anxious to eke out my means to the very last shillings-worth.

I was taking a pair of shoes to be mended at a shop in the Tottenham Court Road when I first encountered the little old man with the yellow face, with whom my life has now become so inextricably entangled. He was standing on the kerb, and staring at the number on the door in a doubtful way, as I opened it. His eyes—they were dull grey eyes, and reddish under the rims—fell to my face, and his countenance immediately assumed an expression of corrugated amiability.

"You come," he said, "apt to the moment. I had forgotten the number of your house. How do you do, Mr. Eden?"

I was a little astonished at his familiar address, for I had never set eyes on the man before. I was a little annoyed, too, at his catching me with my boots under my arm. He noticed my lack of cordiality.

"Wonder who the deuce I am, eh? A friend, let me assure you. I have seen you before, though you haven't seen me. Is there anywhere where I can talk to you?"

I hesitated. The shabbiness of my room upstairs was not a matter for every stranger. "Perhaps," said I, "we might walk down the street. I'm unfortunately prevented—" My gesture explained the sentence before I had spoken it.

"The very thing," he said, and faced this way, and then that. "The street? Which way shall we go?" I slipped my boots down in the passage. "Look here!" he said abruptly; "this business of mine is a rigmarole. Come and lunch with me, Mr. Eden. I'm an old man, a very old man, and not good at explanations, and what with my piping voice and the clatter of the traffic——"

He laid a persuasive skinny hand that trembled a little upon my arm.

I was not so old that an old man might not treat me to a lunch. Yet at the same time I was not altogether pleased by this abrupt invitation. "I had rather——" I began. "But I had rather," he said, catching me up, "and a certain civility is surely due to my grey hairs."

And so I consented, and went with him.

He took me to Blavitiski's; I had to walk slowly to accommodate myself to his paces; and over such a lunch as I had never tasted before, he fended off my leading question, and I took a better note of his appearance. His clean-shaven face was lean and wrinkled, his shrivelled, lips fell over a set of false teeth, and his white hair was thin and rather long; he seemed small to me,—though indeed, most people seemed small to me,—and his shoulders were rounded and bent. And watching him, I could not help but observe that he too was taking note of me, running his eyes, with a curious touch of greed in them, over me, from my broad shoulders to my suntanned hands, and up to my freckled face again. "And now," said he, as we lit our cigarettes, "I must tell you of the business in hand.

"I must tell you, then, that I am an old man, a very old man." He paused momentarily. "And it happens that I have money that I must presently be leaving, and never a child have I to leave it to." I thought of the confidence trick, and resolved I would be on the alert for the vestiges of my five hundred pounds. He proceeded to enlarge on his loneliness, and the trouble he had to find a proper disposition of his money. "I have weighed this plan and that plan, charities, institutions, and scholarships, and libraries, and I have come to this conclusion at last,"—he fixed his eyes on my face,—"that I will find some young fellow, ambitious, pure-minded, and poor, healthy in body and healthy in mind, and, in short, make him my heir, give him all that I have." He repeated, "Give him all that I have. So that he will suddenly be lifted out of all the trouble and struggle in which his sympathies have been educated, to freedom and influence."

I tried to seem disinterested. With a transparent hypocrisy I said, "And you want my help, my professional services maybe, to find that person."

He smiled, and looked at me over his cigarette, and I laughed at his quiet exposure of my modest pretence.

"What a career such a man might have!" he said. "It fills me with envy to think how I have accumulated that another man may spend——

"But there are conditions, of course, burdens to be imposed. He must, for instance, take my name. You cannot expect everything without some return. And I must go into all the circumstances of his life before I can accept him. He must be sound. I must know his heredity, how his parents and grandparents died, have the strictest inquiries made into his private morals."

This modified my secret congratulations a little.

"And do I understand," said I, "that I——"

"Yes," he said, almost fiercely. "You. You."

I answered never a word. My imagination was dancing wildly, my innate scepticism was useless to modify its transports. There was not a particle of gratitude in my mind—I did not know what to say nor how to say it. "But why me in particular?" I said at last.

He had chanced to hear of me from Professor Haslar; he said, as a typically sound and sane young man, and he wished, as far as possible, to leave his money where health and integrity were assured.

That was my first meeting with the little old man. He was mysterious about himself; he would not give his name yet, he said, and after I had answered some questions of his, he left me at the Blavitiski portal. I noticed that he drew a handful of gold coins from his pocket when it came to paying for the lunch. His insistence upon bodily health was curious. In accordance with an arrangement we had made I applied that day for a life policy in the Loyal Insurance Company for a large sum, and I was exhaustively overhauled by the medical advisers of that company in the subsequent week. Even that did not satisfy him, and he insisted I must be re-examined by the great Doctor Henderson.

It was Friday in Whitsun week before he came to a decision. He called me down, quite late in the evening,—nearly nine it was,—from cramming chemical equations for my Preliminary Scientific examination. He was standing in the passage under the feeble gas-lamp, and his face was a grotesque interplay of shadows. He seemed more bowed than when I had first seen him, and his cheeks had sunk in a little.

His voice shook with emotion. "Everything is satisfactory, Mr. Eden," he said. "Everything is quite, quite satisfactory. And this night of all nights, you must dine with me and celebrate your—accession." He was interrupted by a cough. "You won't have long to wait, either," he said, wiping his handkerchief across his lips, and gripping my hand with his long bony claw that was disengaged. "Certainly not very long to wait."

We went into the street and called a cab. I remember every incident of that drive vividly, the swift, easy motion, the vivid contrast of gas and oil and electric light, the crowds of people in the streets, the place in Regent Street to which we went, and the sumptuous dinner we were served with there. I was disconcerted at first by the well-dressed waiter's glances at my rough clothes, bothered by the stones of the olives, but as the champagne warmed my blood, my confidence revived. At first the old man talked of himself. He had already told me his name in the cab; he was Egbert Elvesham, the great philosopher, whose name I had known since I was a lad at school. It seemed incredible to me that this man, whose intelligence had so early dominated mine, this great abstraction, should suddenly realise itself as this decrepit, familiar figure. I daresay every young fellow who has suddenly fallen among celebrities has felt something of my disappointment. He told me now of the future that the feeble streams of his life would presently leave dry for me, houses, copyrights, investments; I had never suspected that philosophers were so rich. He watched me drink and eat with a touch of envy. "What a capacity for living you have!" he said; and then with a sigh, a sigh of relief I could have thought it, "it will not be long."

"Ay," said I, my head swimming now with champagne; "I have a future perhaps—of a passing agreeable sort, thanks to you. I shall now have the honour of your name. But you have a past. Such a past as is worth all my future."

He shook his head and smiled, as I thought, with half sad appreciation of my flattering admiration. "That future," he said, "would you in truth change it?" The waiter came with liqueurs. "You will not perhaps mind taking my name, taking my position, but would you indeed—willingly—take my years?"

"With your achievements," said I gallantly.

He smiled again. "Kummel—both," he said to the waiter, and turned his attention to a little paper packet he had taken from his pocket. "This hour," said he, "this after-dinner hour is the hour of small things. Here is a scrap of my unpublished wisdom." He opened the packet with his shaking yellow fingers, and showed a little pinkish powder on the paper. "This," said he—"well, you must guess what it is. But Kummel—put but a dash of this powder in it—is Himmel."

His large greyish eyes watched mine with an inscrutable expression.

It was a bit of a shock to me to find this great teacher gave his mind to the flavour of liqueurs. However, I feigned an interest in his weakness, for I was drunk enough for such small sycophancy.

He parted the powder between the little glasses, and, rising suddenly, with a strange unexpected dignity, held out his hand towards me. I imitated his action, and the glasses rang. "To a quick succession," said he, and raised his glass towards his lips.

"Not that," I said hastily. "Not that."

He paused with the liqueur at the level of his chin, and his eyes blazing into mine.

"To a long life," said I.

He hesitated. "To a long life," said he, with a sudden bark of laughter, and with eyes fixed on one another we tilted the little glasses. His eyes looked straight into mine, and as I drained the stuff off, I felt a curiously intense sensation. The first touch of it set my brain in a furious tumult; I seemed to feel an actual physical stirring in my skull, and a seething humming filled my ears. I did not notice the flavour in my mouth, the aroma that filled my throat; I saw only the grey intensity of his gaze that burnt into mine. The draught, the mental confusion, the noise and stirring in my head, seemed to last an interminable time.

Curious vague impressions of half-forgotten things danced and vanished on the edge of my consciousness. At last he broke the spell. With a sudden explosive sigh he put down his glass.

"Well?" he said.

"It's glorious," said I, though I had not tasted the stuff.

My head was spinning. I sat down. My brain was chaos. Then my perception grew clear and minute as though I saw things in a concave mirror. His manner seemed to have changed into something nervous and hasty. He pulled out his watch and grimaced at it. "Eleven-seven! And to-night I must— Seven-twenty-five. Waterloo! I must go at once." He called for the bill, and struggled with his coat. Officious waiters came to our assistance. In another moment I was wishing him good-bye, over the apron of a cab, and still with an absurd feeling of minute distinctness, as though—how can I express it?—I not only saw but felt through an inverted opera-glass.

"That stuff," he said. He put his hand to his forehead. "I ought not to have given it to you. It will make your head split to-morrow. Wait a minute. Here." He handed me out a little flat thing like a seidlitz-powder. "Take that in water as you are going to bed. The other thing was a drug. Not till you're ready to go to bed, mind. It will clear your head. That's all. One more shake—Futurus!"

I gripped his shrivelled claw. "Good-bye," he said, and by the droop of his eyelids I judged he too was a little under the influence of that brain-twisting cordial.

He recollected something else with a start, felt in his breast-pocket, and produced another packet, this time a cylinder the size and shape of a shaving-stick. "Here," said he. "I'd almost forgotten. Don't open this until I come to-morrow—but take it now."

It was so heavy that I wellnigh dropped it. "All ri'!" said I, and he grinned at me through the cab window as the cabman flicked his horse into wakefulness. It was a white packet he had given me, with red seals at either end and along its edge. "If this isn't money," said I, "it's platinum or lead."

I stuck it with elaborate care into my pocket, and with a whirling brain walked home through the Regent Street loiterers and the dark back streets beyond Portland Road. I remember the sensations of that walk very vividly, strange as they were. I was still so far myself that I could notice my strange mental state, and wonder whether this stuff I had had was opium—a drug beyond my experience. It is hard now to describe the peculiarity of my mental strangeness—mental doubling vaguely expresses it. As I was walking up Regent Street I found in my mind a queer persuasion that it was Waterloo Station, and had an odd impulse to get into the Polytechnic as a man might get into a train. I put a knuckle in my eye, and it was Regent Street. How can I express it? You see a skilful actor looking quietly at you, he pulls a grimace, and lo!—another person. Is it too extravagant if I tell you that it seemed to me as if Regent Street had, for the moment, done that? Then, being persuaded it was Regent Street again, I was oddly muddled about some fantastic reminiscences that cropped up. "Thirty years ago," thought I, "it was here that I quarrelled with my brother." Then I burst out laughing, to the astonishment and encouragement of a group of night prowlers. Thirty years ago I did not exist, and never in my life had I boasted a brother. The stuff was surely liquid folly, for the poignant regret for that lost brother still clung to me. Along Portland Road the madness took another turn. I began to recall vanished shops, and to compare the street with what it used to be. Confused, troubled thinking is comprehensible enough after the drink I had taken, but what puzzled me were these curiously vivid phantasm memories that had crept into my mind, and not only the memories that had crept in, but also the memories that had slipped out. I stopped opposite Stevens', the natural history dealer's, and cudgelled my brains to think what he had to do with me. A 'bus went by, and sounded exactly like the rumbling of a train. I seemed to be dipping into some dark, remote pit for the recollection. "Of course," said I, at last, "he has promised me three frogs to-morrow. Odd I should have forgotten."

Do they still show children dissolving views? In those I remember one view would begin like a faint ghost, and grow and oust another. In just that way it seemed to me that a ghostly set of new sensations was struggling with those of my ordinary self.

I went on through Euston Road to Tottenham Court Road, puzzled, and a little frightened, and scarcely noticed the unusual way I was taking, for commonly I used to cut through the intervening network of back streets. I turned into University Street, to discover that I had forgotten my number. Only by a strong effort did I recall 11A, and even then it seemed to me that it was a thing some forgotten person had told me. I tried to steady my mind by recalling the incidents of the dinner, and for the life of me I could conjure up no picture of my host's face; I saw him only as a shadowy outline, as one might see oneself reflected in a window through which one was looking. In his place, however, I had a curious exterior vision of myself, sitting at a table, flushed, bright-eyed, and talkative.

"I must take this other powder," said I. "This is getting impossible."

I tried the wrong side of the hall for my candle and the matches, and had a doubt of which landing my room might be on. "I'm drunk," I said, "that's certain," and blundered needlessly on the staircase to sustain the proposition.

At the first glance my room seemed unfamiliar. "What rot!" I said, and stared about me. I seemed to bring myself back by the effort, and the odd phantasmal quality passed into the concrete familiar. There was the old glass still, with my notes on the albumens stuck in the corner of the frame, my old everyday suit of clothes pitched about the floor. And yet it was not so real after all. I felt an idiotic persuasion trying to creep into my mind, as it were, that I was in a railway carriage in a train just stopping, that I was peering out of the window at some unknown station. I gripped the bed-rail firmly to reassure myself. "It's clairvoyance, perhaps," I said. "I must write to the Psychical Research Society."

I put the rouleau on my dressing-table, sat on my bed, and began to take off my boots. It was as if the picture of my present sensations was painted over some other picture that was trying to show through. "Curse it!" said I; "my wits are going, or am I in two places at once?" Half-undressed, I tossed the powder into a glass and drank it off. It effervesced, and became a fluorescent amber colour. Before I was in bed my mind was already tranquillised. I felt the pillow at my cheek, and thereupon I must have fallen asleep.

* * * * *

I awoke abruptly out of a dream of strange beasts, and found myself lying on my back. Probably every one knows that dismal, emotional dream from which one escapes, awake indeed, but strangely cowed. There was a curious taste in my mouth, a tired feeling in my limbs, a sense of cutaneous discomfort. I lay with my head motionless on my pillow, expecting that my feeling of strangeness and terror would pass away, and that I should then doze off again to sleep. But instead of that, my uncanny sensations increased. At first I could perceive nothing wrong about me. There was a faint light in the room, so faint that it was the very next thing to darkness, and the furniture stood out in it as vague blots of absolute darkness. I stared with my eyes just over the bedclothes.

It came into my mind that some one had entered the room to rob me of my rouleau of money, but after lying for some moments, breathing regularly to simulate sleep, I realised this was mere fancy. Nevertheless, the uneasy assurance of something wrong kept fast hold of me. With an effort I raised my head from the pillow, and peered about me at the dark. What it was I could not conceive. I looked at the dim shapes around me, the greater and lesser darknesses that indicated curtains, table, fireplace, bookshelves, and so forth. Then I began to perceive something unfamiliar in the forms of the darkness. Had the bed turned round? Yonder should be the bookshelves, and something shrouded and pallid rose there, something that would not answer to the bookshelves, however I looked at it. It was far too big to be my shirt thrown on a chair.

Overcoming a childish terror, I threw back the bedclothes and thrust my leg out of bed. Instead of coming out of my truckle-bed upon the floor, I found my foot scarcely reached the edge of the mattress. I made another step, as it were, and sat up on the edge of the bed. By the side of my bed should be the candle, and the matches upon the broken chair. I put out my hand and touched—nothing. I waved my hand in the darkness, and it came against some heavy hanging, soft and thick in texture, which gave a rustling noise at my touch. I grasped this and pulled it; it appeared to be a curtain suspended over the head of my bed.

I was now thoroughly awake, and beginning to realise that I was in a strange room. I was puzzled. I tried to recall the overnight circumstances, and I found them now, curiously enough, vivid in my memory: the supper, my reception of the little packages, my wonder whether I was intoxicated, my slow undressing, the coolness to my flushed face of my pillow. I felt a sudden distrust. Was that last night, or the night before? At any rate, this room was strange to me, and I could not imagine how I had got into it. The dim, pallid outline was growing paler, and I perceived it was a window, with the dark shape of an oval toilet-glass against the weak intimation of the dawn that filtered through the blind. I stood up, and was surprised by a curious feeling of weakness and unsteadiness. With trembling hands outstretched, I walked slowly towards the window, getting, nevertheless, a bruise on the knee from a chair by the way. I fumbled round the glass, which was large, with handsome brass sconces, to find the blind cord. I could not find any. By chance I took hold of the tassel, and with the click of a spring the blind ran up.

I found myself looking out upon a scene that was altogether strange to me. The night was overcast, and through the flocculent grey of the heaped clouds there filtered a faint half-light of dawn. Just at the edge of the sky the cloud-canopy had a blood-red rim. Below, everything was dark and indistinct, dim hills in the distance, a vague mass of buildings running up into pinnacles, trees like spilt ink, and below the window a tracery of black bushes and pale grey paths. It was so unfamiliar that for the moment I thought myself still dreaming. I felt the toilet-table; it appeared to be made of some polished wood, and was rather elaborately furnished—there were little cut-glass bottles and a brush upon it. There was also a queer little object, horse-shoe shape it felt, with smooth, hard projections, lying in a saucer. I could find no matches nor candlestick.

I turned my eyes to the room again. Now the blind was up, faint spectres of its furnishing came out of the darkness. There was a huge curtained bed, and the fireplace at its foot had a large white mantel with something of the shimmer of marble.

I leant against the toilet-table, shut my eyes and opened them again, and tried to think. The whole thing was far too real for dreaming. I was inclined to imagine there was still some hiatus in my memory, as a consequence of my draught of that strange liqueur; that I had come into my inheritance perhaps, and suddenly lost my recollection of everything since my good fortune had been announced. Perhaps if I waited a little, things would be clearer to me again. Yet my dinner with old Elvesham was now singularly vivid and recent. The champagne, the observant waiters, the powder, and the liqueurs—I could have staked my soul it all happened a few hours ago.

And then occurred a thing so trivial and yet so terrible to me that I shiver now to think of that moment. I spoke aloud. I said, "How the devil did I get here?" ... And the voice was not my own.

It was not my own, it was thin, the articulation was slurred, the resonance of my facial bones was different. Then, to reassure myself I ran one hand over the other, and felt loose folds of skin, the bony laxity of age. "Surely," I said, in that horrible voice that had somehow established itself in my throat, "surely this thing is a dream!" Almost as quickly as if I did it involuntarily, I thrust my fingers into my mouth. My teeth had gone. My finger-tips ran on the flaccid surface of an even row of shrivelled gums. I was sick with dismay and disgust.

I felt then a passionate desire to see myself, to realise at once in its full horror the ghastly change that had come upon me. I tottered to the mantel, and felt along it for matches. As I did so, a barking cough sprang up in my throat, and I clutched the thick flannel nightdress I found about me. There were no matches there, and I suddenly realised that my extremities were cold. Sniffing and coughing, whimpering a little, perhaps, I fumbled back to bed. "It is surely a dream," I whispered to myself as I clambered back, "surely a dream." It was a senile repetition. I pulled the bedclothes over my shoulders, over my ears, I thrust my withered hand under the pillow, and determined to compose myself to sleep. Of course it was a dream. In the morning the dream would be over, and I should wake up strong and vigorous again to my youth and studies. I shut my eyes, breathed regularly, and, finding myself wakeful, began to count slowly through the powers of three.

But the thing I desired would not come. I could not get to sleep. And the persuasion of the inexorable reality of the change that had happened to me grew steadily. Presently I found myself with my eyes wide open, the powers of three forgotten, and my skinny fingers upon my shrivelled gums, I was, indeed, suddenly and abruptly, an old man. I had in some unaccountable manner fallen through my life and come to old age, in some way I had been cheated of all the best of my life, of love, of struggle, of strength, and hope. I grovelled into the pillow and tried to persuade myself that such hallucination was possible. Imperceptibly, steadily, the dawn grew clearer.

At last, despairing of further sleep, I sat up in bed and looked about me. A chill twilight rendered the whole chamber visible. It was spacious and well-furnished, better furnished than any room I had ever slept in before. A candle and matches became dimly visible upon a little pedestal in a recess. I threw back the bedclothes, and, shivering with the rawness of the early morning, albeit it was summer-time, I got out and lit the candle. Then, trembling horribly, so that the extinguisher rattled on its spike, I tottered to the glass and saw—Elvesham's face! It was none the less horrible because I had already dimly feared as much. He had already seemed physically weak and pitiful to me, but seen now, dressed only in a coarse flannel nightdress, that fell apart and showed the stringy neck, seen now as my own body, I cannot describe its desolate decrepitude. The hollow cheeks, the straggling tail of dirty grey hair, the rheumy bleared eyes, the quivering, shrivelled lips, the lower displaying a gleam of the pink interior lining, and those horrible dark gums showing. You who are mind and body together, at your natural years, cannot imagine what this fiendish imprisonment meant to me. To be young and full of the desire and energy of youth, and to be caught, and presently to be crushed in this tottering ruin of a body...

But I wander from the course of my story. For some time I must have been stunned at this change that had come upon me. It was daylight when I did so far gather myself together as to think. In some inexplicable way I had been changed, though how, short of magic, the thing had been done, I could not say. And as I thought, the diabolical ingenuity of Elvesham came home to me. It seemed plain to me that as I found myself in his, so he must be in possession of my body, of my strength, that is, and my future. But how to prove it? Then, as I thought, the thing became so incredible, even to me, that my mind reeled, and I had to pinch myself, to feel my toothless gums, to see myself in the glass, and touch the things about me, before I could steady myself to face the facts again. Was all life hallucination? Was I indeed Elvesham, and he me? Had I been dreaming of Eden overnight? Was there any Eden? But if I was Elvesham, I should remember where I was on the previous morning, the name of the town in which I lived, what happened before the dream began. I struggled with my thoughts. I recalled the queer doubleness of my memories overnight. But now my mind was clear. Not the ghost of any memories but those proper to Eden could I raise.

"This way lies insanity!" I cried in my piping voice. I staggered to my feet, dragged my feeble, heavy limbs to the washhand-stand, and plunged my grey head into a basin of cold water. Then, towelling myself, I tried again. It was no good. I felt beyond all question that I was indeed Eden, not Elvesham. But Eden in Elvesham's body!

Had I been a man of any other age, I might have given myself up to my fate as one enchanted. But in these sceptical days miracles do not pass current. Here was some trick of psychology. What a drug and a steady stare could do, a drug and a steady stare, or some similar treatment, could surely undo. Men have lost their memories before. But to exchange memories as one does umbrellas! I laughed. Alas! not a healthy laugh, but a wheezing, senile titter. I could have fancied old Elvesham laughing at my plight, and a gust of petulant anger, unusual to me, swept across my feelings. I began dressing eagerly in the clothes I found lying about on the floor, and only realised when I was dressed that it was an evening suit I had assumed. I opened the wardrobe and found some more ordinary clothes, a pair of plaid trousers, and an old-fashioned dressing-gown. I put a venerable smoking-cap on my venerable head, and, coughing a little from my exertions, tottered out upon the landing.

It was then, perhaps, a quarter to six, and the blinds were closely drawn and the house quite silent. The landing was a spacious one, a broad, richly-carpeted staircase went down into the darkness of the hall below, and before me a door ajar showed me a writing-desk, a revolving bookcase, the back of a study chair, and a fine array of bound books, shelf upon shelf.

"My study," I mumbled, and walked across the landing. Then at the sound of my voice a thought struck me, and I went back to the bedroom and put in the set of false teeth. They slipped in with the ease of old, habit. "That's better," said I, gnashing them, and so returned to the study.

The drawers of the writing-desk were locked. Its revolving top was also locked. I could see no indications of the keys, and there were none in the pockets of my trousers. I shuffled back at once to the bedroom, and went through the dress suit, and afterwards the pockets of all the garments I could find. I was very eager, and one might have imagined that burglars had been at work, to see my room when I had done. Not only were there no keys to be found, but not a coin, nor a scrap of paper—save only the receipted bill of the overnight dinner.

A curious weariness asserted itself. I sat down and stared at the garments flung here and there, their pockets turned inside out. My first frenzy had already flickered out. Every moment I was beginning to realise the immense intelligence of the plans of my enemy, to see more and more clearly the hopelessness of my position. With an effort I rose and hurried hobbling into the study again. On the staircase was a housemaid pulling up the blinds. She stared, I think, at the expression of my face. I shut the door of the study behind me, and, seizing a poker, began an attack upon the desk. That is how they found me. The cover of the desk was split, the lock smashed, the letters torn out of the pigeon-holes, and tossed about the room. In my senile rage I had flung about the pens and other such light stationery, and overturned the ink. Moreover, a large vase upon the mantel had got broken—I do not know how. I could find no cheque-book, no money, no indications of the slightest use for the recovery of my body. I was battering madly at the drawers, when the butler, backed by two women-servants, intruded upon me.

* * * * *

That simply is the story of my change. No one will believe my frantic assertions. I am treated as one demented, and even at this moment I am under restraint. But I am sane, absolutely sane, and to prove it I have sat down to write this story minutely as the things happened to me. I appeal to the reader, whether there is any trace of insanity in the style or method, of the story he has been reading. I am a young man locked away in an old man's body. But the clear fact is incredible to everyone. Naturally I appear demented to those who will not believe this, naturally I do not know the names of my secretaries, of the doctors who come to see me, of my servants and neighbours, of this town (wherever it is) where I find myself. Naturally I lose myself in my own house, and suffer inconveniences of every sort. Naturally I ask the oddest questions. Naturally I weep and cry out, and have paroxysms of despair. I have no money and no cheque-book. The bank will not recognise my signature, for I suppose that, allowing for the feeble muscles I now have, my handwriting is still Eden's. These people about me will not let me go to the bank personally. It seems, indeed, that there is no bank in this town, and that I have an account in some part of London. It seems that Elvesham kept the name of his solicitor secret from all his household. I can ascertain nothing. Elvesham was, of course, a profound student of mental science, and all my declarations of the facts of the case merely confirm the theory that my insanity is the outcome of overmuch brooding upon psychology. Dreams of the personal identity indeed! Two days ago I was a healthy youngster, with all life before me; now I am a furious old man, unkempt, and desperate, and miserable, prowling about a great, luxurious, strange house, watched, feared, and avoided as a lunatic by everyone about me. And in London is Elvesham beginning life again in a vigorous body, and with all the accumulated knowledge and wisdom of threescore and ten. He has stolen my life.

What has happened I do not clearly know. In the study are volumes of manuscript notes referring chiefly to the psychology of memory, and parts of what may be either calculations or ciphers in symbols absolutely strange to me. In some passages there are indications that he was also occupied with the philosophy of mathematics. I take it he has transferred the whole of his memories, the accumulation that makes up his personality, from this old withered brain of his to mine, and, similarly, that he has transferred mine to his discarded tenement. Practically, that is, he has changed bodies. But how such a change may be possible is without the range of my philosophy. I have been a materialist for all my thinking life, but here, suddenly, is a clear case of man's detachability from matter.

One desperate experiment I am about to try. I sit writing here before putting the matter to issue. This morning, with the help of a table-knife that I had secreted at breakfast, I succeeded in breaking open a fairly obvious secret drawer in this wrecked writing-desk. I discovered nothing save a little green glass phial containing a white powder. Round the neck of the phial was a label, and thereon was written this one word, "Release." This may be—is most probably—poison. I can understand Elvesham placing poison in my way, and I should be sure that it was his intention so to get rid of the only living witness against him, were it not for this careful concealment. The man has practically solved the problem of immortality. Save for the spite of chance, he will live in my body until it has aged, and then, again, throwing that aside, he will assume some other victim's youth and strength. When one remembers his heartlessness, it is terrible to think of the ever-growing experience that... How long has he been leaping from body to body?... But I tire of writing. The powder appears to be soluble in water. The taste is not unpleasant.

* * * * *

There the narrative found upon Mr. Elvesham's desk ends. His dead body lay between the desk and the chair. The latter had been pushed back, probably by his last convulsions. The story was written in pencil and in a crazy hand, quite unlike his usual minute characters. There remain only two curious facts to record. Indisputably there was some connection between Eden and Elvesham, since the whole of Elvesham's property was bequeathed to the young man. But he never inherited. When Elvesham committed suicide, Eden was, strangely enough, already dead. Twenty-four hours before, he had been knocked down by a cab and killed instantly, at the crowded crossing at the intersection of Gower Street and Euston Road. So that the only human being who could have thrown light upon this fantastic narrative is beyond the reach of questions. Without further comment I leave this extraordinary matter to the reader's individual judgment.

XII.

UNDER THE KNIFE.

"What if I die under it?" The thought recurred again and again, as I walked home from Haddon's. It was a purely personal question. I was spared the deep anxieties of a married man, and I knew there were few of my intimate friends but would find my death troublesome chiefly on account of their duty of regret. I was surprised indeed, and perhaps a little humiliated, as I turned the matter over, to think how few could possibly exceed the conventional requirement. Things came before me stripped of glamour, in a clear dry light, during that walk from Haddon's house over Primrose Hill. There were the friends of my youth: I perceived now that our affection was a tradition, which we foregathered rather laboriously to maintain. There were the rivals and helpers of my later career: I suppose I had been cold-blooded or undemonstrative—one perhaps implies the other. It may be that even the capacity for friendship is a question of physique. There had been a time in my own life when I had grieved bitterly enough at the loss of a friend; but as I walked home that afternoon the emotional side of my imagination was dormant. I could not pity myself, nor feel sorry for my friends, nor conceive of them as grieving for me.

I was interested in this deadness of my emotional nature—no doubt a concomitant of my stagnating physiology; and my thoughts wandered off along the line it suggested. Once before, in my hot youth, I had suffered a sudden loss of blood, and had been within an ace of death. I remembered now that my affections as well as my passions had drained out of me, leaving scarce anything but a tranquil resignation, a dreg of self-pity. It had been weeks before the old ambitions and tendernesses and all the complex moral interplay of a man had reasserted themselves. It occurred to me that the real meaning of this numbness might be a gradual slipping away from the pleasure-pain guidance of the animal man. It has been proven, I take it, as thoroughly as anything can be proven in this world, that the higher emotions, the moral feelings, even the subtle unselfishness of love, are evolved from the elemental desires and fears of the simple animal: they are the harness in which man's mental freedom goes. And it may be that as death overshadows us, as our possibility of acting diminishes, this complex growth of balanced impulse, propensity and aversion, whose interplay inspires our acts, goes with it. Leaving what?

I was suddenly brought back to reality by an imminent collision with the butcher-boy's tray. I found that I was crossing the bridge over the Regent's Park Canal, which runs parallel with that in the Zoological Gardens. The boy in blue had been looking over his shoulder at a black barge advancing slowly, towed by a gaunt white horse. In the Gardens a nurse was leading three happy little children over the bridge. The trees were bright green; the spring hopefulness was still unstained by the dusts of summer; the sky in the water was bright and clear, but broken by long waves, by quivering bands of black, as the barge drove through. The breeze was stirring; but it did not stir me as the spring breeze used to do.

Was this dulness of feeling in itself an anticipation? It was curious that I could reason and follow out a network of suggestion as clearly as ever: so, at least, it seemed to me. It was calmness rather than dulness that was coming upon me. Was there any ground for the relief in the presentiment of death? Did a man near to death begin instinctively to withdraw himself from the meshes of matter and sense, even before the cold hand was laid upon his? I felt strangely isolated—isolated without regret—from the life and existence about me. The children playing in the sun and gathering strength and experience for the business of life, the park-keeper gossiping with a nursemaid, the nursing mother, the young couple intent upon each other as they passed me, the trees by the wayside spreading new pleading leaves to the sunlight, the stir in their branches—I had been part of it all, but I had nearly done with it now.

Some way down the Broad Walk I perceived that I was tired, and that my feet were heavy. It was hot that afternoon, and I turned aside and sat down on one of the green chairs that line the way. In a minute I had dozed into a dream, and the tide of my thoughts washed up a vision of the resurrection. I was still sitting in the chair, but I thought myself actually dead, withered, tattered, dried, one eye (I saw) pecked out by birds. "Awake!" cried a voice; and incontinently the dust of the path and the mould under the grass became insurgent. I had never before thought of Regent's Park as a cemetery, but now, through the trees, stretching as far as eye could see, I beheld a flat plain of writhing graves and heeling tombstones. There seemed to be some trouble: the rising dead appeared to stifle as they struggled upward, they bled in their struggles, the red flesh was torn away from the white bones. "Awake!" cried a voice; but I determined I would not rise to such horrors. "Awake!" They would not let me alone. "Wake up!" said an angry voice. A cockney angel! The man who sells the tickets was shaking me, demanding my penny.

I paid my penny, pocketed my ticket, yawned, stretched my legs, and, feeling now rather less torpid, got up and walked on towards Langham Place. I speedily lost myself again in a shifting maze of thoughts about death. Going across Marylebone Road into that crescent at the end of Langham Place, I had the narrowest escape from the shaft of a cab, and went on my way with a palpitating heart and a bruised shoulder. It struck me that it would have been curious if my meditations on my death on the morrow had led to my death that day.

But I will not weary you with more of my experiences that day and the next. I knew more and more certainly that I should die under the operation; at times I think I was inclined to pose to myself. The doctors were coming at eleven, and I did not get up. It seemed scarce worth while to trouble about washing and dressing, and though I read my newspapers and the letters that came by the first post, I did not find them very interesting. There was a friendly note from Addison, my old school-friend, calling my attention to two discrepancies and a printer's error in my new book, with one from Langridge venting some vexation over Minton. The rest were business communications. I breakfasted in bed. The glow of pain at my side seemed more massive. I knew it was pain, and yet, if you can understand, I did not find it very painful. I had been awake and hot and thirsty in the night, but in the morning bed felt comfortable. In the night-time I had lain thinking of things that were past; in the morning I dozed over the question of immortality. Haddon came, punctual to the minute, with a neat black bag; and Mowbray soon followed. Their arrival stirred me up a little. I began to take a more personal interest in the proceedings. Haddon moved the little octagonal table close to the bedside, and, with his broad back to me, began taking things out of his bag. I heard the light click of steel upon steel. My imagination, I found, was not altogether stagnant. "Will you hurt me much?" I said in an off-hand tone.

"Not a bit," Haddon answered over his shoulder. "We shall chloroform you. Your heart's as sound as a bell." And as he spoke, I had a whiff of the pungent sweetness of the anaesthetic.

They stretched me out, with a convenient exposure of my side, and, almost before I realised what was happening, the chloroform was being administered. It stings the nostrils, and there is a suffocating sensation at first. I knew I should die—that this was the end of consciousness for me. And suddenly I felt that I was not prepared for death: I had a vague sense of a duty overlooked—I knew not what. What was it I had not done? I could think of nothing more to do, nothing desirable left in life; and yet I had the strangest disinclination to death. And the physical sensation was painfully oppressive. Of course the doctors did not know they were going to kill me. Possibly I struggled. Then I fell motionless, and a great silence, a monstrous silence, and an impenetrable blackness came upon me.

There must have been an interval of absolute unconsciousness, seconds or minutes. Then with a chilly, unemotional clearness, I perceived that I was not yet dead. I was still in my body; but all the multitudinous sensations that come sweeping from it to make up the background of consciousness had gone, leaving me free of it all. No, not free of it all; for as yet something still held me to the poor stark flesh upon the bed—held me, yet not so closely that I did not feel myself external to it, independent of it, straining away from it. I do not think I saw, I do not think I heard; but I perceived all that was going on, and it was as if I both heard and saw. Haddon was bending over me, Mowbray behind me; the scalpel—it was a large scalpel—was cutting my flesh at the side under the flying ribs. It was interesting to see myself cut like cheese, without a pang, without even a qualm. The interest was much of a quality with that one might feel in a game of chess between strangers. Haddon's face was firm and his hand steady; but I was surprised to perceive (how I know not) that he was feeling the gravest doubt as to his own wisdom in the conduct of the operation.

Mowbray's thoughts, too, I could see. He was thinking that Haddon's manner showed too much of the specialist. New suggestions came up like bubbles through a stream of frothing meditation, and burst one after another in the little bright spot of his consciousness. He could not help noticing and admiring Haddon's swift dexterity, in spite of his envious quality and his disposition to detract. I saw my liver exposed. I was puzzled at my own condition. I did not feel that I was dead, but I was different in some way from my living self. The grey depression, that had weighed on me for a year or more and coloured all my thoughts, was gone. I perceived and thought without any emotional tint at all. I wondered if everyone perceived things in this way under chloroform, and forgot it again when he came out of it. It would be inconvenient to look into some heads, and not forget.

Although I did not think that I was dead, I still perceived quite clearly that I was soon to die. This brought me back to the consideration of Haddon's proceedings. I looked into his mind, and saw that he was afraid of cutting a branch of the portal vein. My attention was distracted from details by the curious changes going on in his mind. His consciousness was like the quivering little spot of light which is thrown by the mirror of a galvanometer. His thoughts ran under it like a stream, some through the focus bright and distinct, some shadowy in the half-light of the edge. Just now the little glow was steady; but the least movement on Mowbray's part, the slightest sound from outside, even a faint difference in the slow movement of the living flesh he was cutting, set the light-spot shivering and spinning. A new sense-impression came rushing up through the flow of thoughts; and lo! the light-spot jerked away towards it, swifter than a frightened fish. It was wonderful to think that upon that unstable, fitful thing depended all the complex motions of the man; that for the next five minutes, therefore, my life hung upon its movements. And he was growing more and more nervous in his work. It was as if a little picture of a cut vein grew brighter, and struggled to oust from his brain another picture of a cut falling short of the mark. He was afraid: his dread of cutting too little was battling with his dread of cutting too far.

Then, suddenly, like an escape of water from under a lock-gate, a great uprush of horrible realisation set all his thoughts swirling, and simultaneously I perceived that the vein was cut. He started back with a hoarse exclamation, and I saw the brown-purple blood gather in a swift bead, and run trickling. He was horrified. He pitched the red-stained scalpel on to the octagonal table; and instantly both doctors flung themselves upon me, making hasty and ill-conceived efforts to remedy the disaster. "Ice!" said Mowbray, gasping. But I knew that I was killed, though my body still clung to me.

I will not describe their belated endeavours to save me, though I perceived every detail. My perceptions were sharper and swifter than they had ever been in life; my thoughts rushed through my mind with incredible swiftness, but with perfect definition. I can only compare their crowded clarity to the effects of a reasonable dose of opium. In a moment it would all be over, and I should be free. I knew I was immortal, but what would happen I did not know. Should I drift off presently, like a puff of smoke from a gun, in some kind of half-material body, an attenuated version of my material self? Should I find myself suddenly among the innumerable hosts of the dead, and know the world about me for the phantasmagoria it had always seemed? Should I drift to some spiritualistic séance, and there make foolish, incomprehensible attempts to affect a purblind medium? It was a state of unemotional curiosity, of colourless expectation. And then I realised a growing stress upon me, a feeling as though some huge human magnet was drawing me upward out of my body. The stress grew and grew. I seemed an atom for which monstrous forces were fighting. For one brief, terrible moment sensation came back to me. That feeling of falling headlong which comes in nightmares, that feeling a thousand times intensified, that and a black horror swept across my thoughts in a torrent. Then the two doctors, the naked body with its cut side, the little room, swept away from under me and vanished, as a speck of foam vanishes down an eddy.

I was in mid-air. Far below was the West End of London, receding rapidly,—for I seemed to be flying swiftly upward,—and as it receded, passing westward like a panorama. I could see, through the faint haze of smoke, the innumerable roofs chimney-set, the narrow roadways, stippled with people and conveyances, the little specks of squares, and the church steeples like thorns sticking out of the fabric. But it spun away as the earth rotated on its axis, and in a few seconds (as it seemed) I was over the scattered clumps of town about Ealing, the little Thames a thread of blue to the south, and the Chiltern Hills and the North Downs coming up like the rim of a basin, far away and faint with haze. Up I rushed. And at first I had not the faintest conception what this headlong rush upward could mean.

Every moment the circle of scenery beneath me grew wider and wider, and the details of town and field, of hill and valley, got more and more hazy and pale and indistinct, a luminous grey was mingled more and more with the blue of the hills and the green of the open meadows; and a little patch of cloud, low and far to the west, shone ever more dazzlingly white. Above, as the veil of atmosphere between myself and outer space grew thinner, the sky, which had been a fair springtime blue at first, grew deeper and richer in colour, passing steadily through the intervening shades, until presently it was as dark as the blue sky of midnight, and presently as black as the blackness of a frosty starlight, and at last as black as no blackness I had ever beheld. And first one star, and then many, and at last an innumerable host broke out upon the sky: more stars than anyone has ever seen from the face of the earth. For the blueness of the sky in the light of the sun and stars sifted and spread abroad blindingly: there is diffused light even in the darkest skies of winter, and we do not see the stars by day only because of the dazzling irradiation of the sun. But now I saw things—I know not how; assuredly with no mortal eyes—and that defect of bedazzlement blinded me no longer. The sun was incredibly strange and wonderful. The body of it was a disc of blinding white light: not yellowish, as it seems to those who live upon the earth, but livid white, all streaked with scarlet streaks and rimmed about with a fringe of writhing tongues of red fire. And shooting half-way across the heavens from either side of it and brighter than the Milky Way, were two pinions of silver white, making it look more like those winged globes I have seen in Egyptian sculpture than anything else I can remember upon earth. These I knew for the solar corona, though I had never seen anything of it but a picture during the days of my earthly life.

When my attention came back to the earth again, I saw that it had fallen very far away from me. Field and town were long since indistinguishable, and all the varied hues of the country were merging into a uniform bright grey, broken only by the brilliant white of the clouds that lay scattered in flocculent masses over Ireland and the west of England. For now I could see the outlines of the north of France and Ireland, and all this Island of Britain, save where Scotland passed over the horizon to the north, or where the coast was blurred or obliterated by cloud. The sea was a dull grey, and darker than the land; and the whole panorama was rotating slowly towards the east.

All this had happened so swiftly that until I was some thousand miles or so from the earth I had no thought for myself. But now I perceived I had neither hands nor feet, neither parts nor organs, and that I felt neither alarm nor pain. All about me I perceived that the vacancy (for I had already left the air behind) was cold beyond the imagination of man; but it troubled me not. The sun's rays shot through the void, powerless to light or heat until they should strike on matter in their course. I saw things with a serene self-forgetfulness, even as if I were God. And down below there, rushing away from me,—countless miles in a second,—where a little dark spot on the grey marked the position of London, two doctors were struggling to restore life to the poor hacked and outworn shell I had abandoned. I felt then such release, such serenity as I can compare to no mortal delight I have ever known.

It was only after I had perceived all these things that the meaning of that headlong rush of the earth grew into comprehension. Yet it was so simple, so obvious, that I was amazed at my never anticipating the thing that was happening to me. I had suddenly been cut adrift from matter: all that was material of me was there upon earth, whirling away through space, held to the earth by gravitation, partaking of the earth-inertia, moving in its wreath of epicycles round the sun, and with the sun and the planets on their vast march through space. But the immaterial has no inertia, feels nothing of the pull of matter for matter: where it parts from its garment of flesh, there it remains (so far as space concerns it any longer) immovable in space. I was not leaving the earth: the earth was leaving me, and not only the earth but the whole solar system was streaming past. And about me in space, invisible to me, scattered in the wake of the earth upon its journey, there must be an innumerable multitude of souls, stripped like myself of the material, stripped like myself of the passions of the individual and the generous emotions of the gregarious brute, naked intelligences, things of new-born wonder and thought, marvelling at the strange release that had suddenly come on them!

As I receded faster and faster from the strange white sun in the black heavens, and from the broad and shining earth upon which my being had begun, I seemed to grow in some incredible manner vast: vast as regards this world I had left, vast as regards the moments and periods of a human life. Very soon I saw the full circle of the earth, slightly gibbous, like the moon when she nears her full, but very large; and the silvery shape of America was now in the noonday blaze wherein (as it seemed) little England had been basking but a few minutes ago. At first the earth was large, and shone in the heavens, filling a great part of them; but every moment she grew smaller and more distant. As she shrank, the broad moon in its third quarter crept into view over the rim of her disc. I looked for the constellations. Only that part of Aries directly behind the sun and the Lion, which the earth covered, were hidden. I recognised the tortuous, tattered band of the Milky Way with Vega very bright between sun and earth; and Sirius and Orion shone splendid against the unfathomable blackness in the opposite quarter of the heavens. The Pole Star was overhead, and the Great Bear hung over the circle of the earth. And away beneath and beyond the shining corona of the sun were strange groupings of stars I had never seen in my life—notably a dagger-shaped group that I knew for the Southern Cross. All these were no larger than when they had shone on earth, but the little stars that one scarce sees shone now against the setting of black vacancy as brightly as the first-magnitudes had done, while the larger worlds were points of indescribable glory and colour. Aldebaran was a spot of blood-red fire, and Sirius condensed to one point the light of innumerable sapphires. And they shone steadily: they did not scintillate, they were calmly glorious. My impressions had an adamantine hardness and brightness: there was no blurring softness, no atmosphere, nothing but infinite darkness set with the myriads of these acute and brilliant points and specks of light. Presently, when I looked again, the little earth seemed no bigger than the sun, and it dwindled and turned as I looked, until in a second's space (as it seemed to me), it was halved; and so it went on swiftly dwindling. Far away in the opposite direction, a little pinkish pin's head of light, shining steadily, was the planet Mars. I swam motionless in vacancy, and, without a trace of terror or astonishment, watched the speck of cosmic dust we call the world fall away from me.

Presently it dawned upon me that my sense of duration had changed; that my mind was moving not faster but infinitely slower, that between each separate impression there was a period of many days. The moon spun once round the earth as I noted this; and I perceived clearly the motion of Mars in his orbit. Moreover, it appeared as if the time between thought and thought grew steadily greater, until at last a thousand years was but a moment in my perception.

At first the constellations had shone motionless against the black background of infinite space; but presently it seemed as though the group of stars about Hercules and the Scorpion was contracting, while Orion and Aldebaran and their neighbours were scattering apart. Flashing suddenly out of the darkness there came a flying multitude of particles of rock, glittering like dust-specks in a sunbeam, and encompassed in a faintly luminous cloud. They swirled all about me, and vanished again in a twinkling far behind. And then I saw that a bright spot of light, that shone a little to one side of my path, was growing very rapidly larger, and perceived that it was the planet Saturn rushing towards me. Larger and larger it grew, swallowing up the heavens behind it, and hiding every moment a fresh multitude, of stars. I perceived its flattened, whirling body, its disc-like belt, and seven of its little satellites. It grew and grew, till it towered enormous; and then I plunged amid a streaming multitude of clashing stones and dancing dust-particles and gas-eddies, and saw for a moment the mighty triple belt like three concentric arches of moonlight above me, its shadow black on the boiling tumult below. These things happened in one-tenth of the time it takes to tell them. The planet went by like a flash of lightning; for a few seconds it blotted out the sun, and there and then became a mere black, dwindling, winged patch against the light. The earth, the mother mote of my being, I could no longer see.

So with a stately swiftness, in the profoundest silence, the solar system fell from me as it had been a garment, until the sun was a mere star amid the multitude of stars, with its eddy of planet-specks lost in the confused glittering of the remoter light. I was no longer a denizen of the solar system: I had come to the outer Universe, I seemed to grasp and comprehend the whole world of matter. Ever more swiftly the stars closed in about the spot where Antares and Vega had vanished in a phosphorescent haze, until that part of the sky had the semblance of a whirling mass of nebulae, and ever before me yawned vaster gaps of vacant blackness, and the stars shone fewer and fewer. It seemed as if I moved towards a point between Orion's belt and sword; and the void about that region opened vaster and vaster every second, an incredible gulf of nothingness into which I was falling. Faster and ever faster the universe rushed by, a hurry of whirling motes at last, speeding silently into the void. Stars glowing brighter and brighter, with their circling planets catching the light in a ghostly fashion as I neared them, shone out and vanished again into inexistence; faint comets, clusters of meteorites, winking specks of matter, eddying light-points, whizzed past, some perhaps a hundred millions of miles or so from me at most, few nearer, travelling with unimaginable rapidity, shooting constellations, momentary darts of fire, through that black, enormous night. More than anything else it was like a dusty draught, sunbeam-lit. Broader and wider and deeper grew the starless space, the vacant Beyond, into which I was being drawn. At last a quarter of the heavens was black and blank, and the whole headlong rush of stellar universe closed in behind me like a veil of light that is gathered together. It drove away from me like a monstrous jack-o'-lantern driven by the wind. I had come out into the wilderness of space. Ever the vacant blackness grew broader, until the hosts of the stars seemed only like a swarm of fiery specks hurrying away from me, inconceivably remote, and the darkness, the nothingness and emptiness, was about me on every side. Soon the little universe of matter, the cage of points in which I had begun to be, was dwindling, now to a whirling disc of luminous glittering, and now to one minute disc of hazy light. In a little while it would shrink to a point, and at last would vanish altogether.

Suddenly feeling came back to me—feeling in the shape of overwhelming terror; such a dread of those dark vastitudes as no words can describe, a passionate resurgence of sympathy and social desire. Were there other souls, invisible to me as I to them, about me in the blackness? or was I indeed, even as I felt, alone? Had I passed out of being into something that was neither being nor not-being? The covering of the body, the covering of matter, had been torn from me, and the hallucinations of companionship and security. Everything was black and silent. I had ceased to be. I was nothing. There was nothing, save only that infinitesimal dot of light that dwindled in the gulf. I strained myself to hear and see, and for a while there was naught but infinite silence, intolerable darkness, horror, and despair.

Then I saw that about the spot of light into which the whole world of matter had shrunk there was a faint glow. And in a band on either side of that the darkness was not absolute. I watched it for ages, as it seemed to me, and through the long waiting the haze grew imperceptibly more distinct. And then about the band appeared an irregular cloud of the faintest, palest brown. I felt a passionate impatience; but the things grew brighter so slowly that they scarce seemed to change. What was unfolding itself? What was this strange reddish dawn in the interminable night of space?

The cloud's shape was grotesque. It seemed to be looped along its lower side into four projecting masses, and, above, it ended in a straight line. What phantom was it? I felt assured I had seen that figure before; but I could not think what, nor where, nor when it was. Then the realisation rushed upon me. It was a clenched Hand. I was alone in space, alone with this huge, shadowy Hand, upon which the whole Universe of Matter lay like an unconsidered speck of dust. It seemed as though I watched it through vast periods of time. On the forefinger glittered a ring; and the universe from which I had come was but a spot of light upon the ring's curvature. And the thing that the hand gripped had the likeness of a black rod. Through a long eternity I watched this Hand, with the ring and the rod, marvelling and fearing and waiting helplessly on what might follow. It seemed as though nothing could follow: that I should watch for ever, seeing only the Hand and the thing it held, and understanding nothing of its import. Was the whole universe but a refracting speck upon some greater Being? Were our worlds but the atoms of another universe, and those again of another, and so on through an endless progression? And what was I? Was I indeed immaterial? A vague persuasion of a body gathering about me came into my suspense. The abysmal darkness about the Hand filled with impalpable suggestions, with uncertain, fluctuating shapes.

Then, suddenly, came a sound, like the sound of a tolling bell: faint, as if infinitely far; muffled, as though heard through thick swathings of darkness: a deep, vibrating resonance, with vast gulfs of silence between each stroke. And the Hand appeared to tighten on the rod. And I saw far above the Hand, towards the apex of the darkness, a circle of dim phosphorescence, a ghostly sphere whence these sounds came throbbing; and at the last stroke the Hand vanished, for the hour had come, and I heard a noise of many waters. But the black rod remained as a great band across the sky. And then a voice, which seemed to run to the uttermost parts of space, spoke, saying, "There will be no more pain."

At that an almost intolerable gladness and radiance rushed in upon me, and I saw the circle shining white and bright, and the rod black and shining, and many things else distinct and clear. And the circle was the face of the clock, and the rod the rail of my bed. Haddon was standing at the foot, against the rail, with a small pair of scissors on his fingers; and the hands of my clock on the mantel over his shoulder were clasped together over the hour of twelve. Mowbray was washing something in a basin at the octagonal table, and at my side I felt a subdued feeling that could scarce be spoken of as pain.

The operation had not killed me. And I perceived, suddenly, that the dull melancholy of half a year was lifted from my mind.

XIII.

THE SEA RAIDERS.

I.

Until the extraordinary affair at Sidmouth, the peculiar species Haploteuthis ferox was known to science only generically, on the strength of a half-digested tentacle obtained near the Azores, and a decaying body pecked by birds and nibbled by fish, found early in 1896 by Mr. Jennings, near Land's End.

In no department of zoological science, indeed, are we quite so much in the dark as with regard to the deep-sea cephalopods. A mere accident, for instance, it was that led to the Prince of Monaco's discovery of nearly a dozen new forms in the summer of 1895, a discovery in which the before-mentioned tentacle was included. It chanced that a cachalot was killed off Terceira by some sperm whalers, and in its last struggles charged almost to the Prince's yacht, missed it, rolled under, and died within twenty yards of his rudder. And in its agony it threw up a number of large objects, which the Prince, dimly perceiving they were strange and important, was, by a happy expedient, able to secure before they sank. He set his screws in motion, and kept them circling in the vortices thus created until a boat could be lowered. And these specimens were whole cephalopods and fragments of cephalopods, some of gigantic proportions, and almost all of them unknown to science!

It would seem, indeed, that these large and agile creatures, living in the middle depths of the sea, must, to a large extent, for ever remain unknown to us, since under water they are too nimble for nets, and it is only by such rare, unlooked-for accidents that specimens can be obtained. In the case of Haploteuthis ferox, for instance, we are still altogether ignorant of its habitat, as ignorant as we are of the breeding-ground of the herring or the sea-ways of the salmon. And zoologists are altogether at a loss to account for its sudden appearance on our coast. Possibly it was the stress of a hunger migration that drove it hither out of the deep. But it will be, perhaps, better to avoid necessarily inconclusive discussion, and to proceed at once with our narrative.

The first human being to set eyes upon a living Haploteuthis—the first human being to survive, that is, for there can be little doubt now that the wave of bathing fatalities and boating accidents that travelled along the coast of Cornwall and Devon in early May was due to this cause—was a retired tea-dealer of the name of Fison, who was stopping at a Sidmouth boarding-house. It was in the afternoon, and he was walking along the cliff path between Sidmouth and Ladram Bay. The cliffs in this direction are very high, but down the red face of them in one place a kind of ladder staircase has been made. He was near this when his attention was attracted by what at first he thought to be a cluster of birds struggling over a fragment of food that caught the sunlight, and glistened pinkish-white. The tide was right out, and this object was not only far below him, but remote across a broad waste of rock reefs covered with dark seaweed and interspersed with silvery shining tidal pools. And he was, moreover, dazzled by the brightness of the further water.

In a minute, regarding this again, he perceived that his judgment was in fault, for over this struggle circled a number of birds, jackdaws and gulls for the most part, the latter gleaming blindingly when the sunlight smote their wings, and they seemed minute in comparison with it. And his curiosity was, perhaps, aroused all the more strongly because of his first insufficient explanations.

As he had nothing better to do than amuse himself, he decided to make this object, whatever it was, the goal of his afternoon walk, instead of Ladram Bay, conceiving it might perhaps be a great fish of some sort, stranded by some chance, and flapping about in its distress. And so he hurried down the long steep ladder, stopping at intervals of thirty feet or so to take breath and scan the mysterious movement.

At the foot of the cliff he was, of course, nearer his object than he had been; but, on the other hand, it now came up against the incandescent sky, beneath the sun, so as to seem dark and indistinct. Whatever was pinkish of it was now hidden by a skerry of weedy boulders. But he perceived that it was made up of seven rounded bodies distinct or connected, and that the birds kept up a constant croaking and screaming, but seemed afraid to approach it too closely.

Mr. Fison, torn by curiosity, began picking his way across the wave-worn rocks, and finding the wet seaweed that covered them thickly rendered them extremely slippery, he stopped, removed his shoes and socks, and rolled his trousers above his knees. His object was, of course, merely to avoid stumbling into the rocky pools about him, and perhaps he was rather glad, as all men are, of an excuse to resume, even for a moment, the sensations of his boyhood. At any rate, it is to this, no doubt, that he owes his life.

He approached his mark with all the assurance which the absolute security of this country against all forms of animal life gives its inhabitants. The round bodies moved to and fro, but it was only when he surmounted the skerry of boulders I have mentioned that he realised the horrible nature of the discovery. It came upon him with some suddenness.

The rounded bodies fell apart as he came into sight over the ridge, and displayed the pinkish object to be the partially devoured body of a human being, but whether of a man or woman he was unable to say. And the rounded bodies were new and ghastly-looking creatures, in shape somewhat resembling an octopus, with huge and very long and flexible tentacles, coiled copiously on the ground. The skin had a glistening texture, unpleasant to see, like shiny leather. The downward bend of the tentacle-surrounded mouth, the curious excrescence at the bend, the tentacles, and the large intelligent eyes, gave the creatures a grotesque suggestion of a face. They were the size of a fair-sized swine about the body, and the tentacles seemed to him to be many feet in length. There were, he thinks, seven or eight at least of the creatures. Twenty yards beyond them, amid the surf of the now returning tide, two others were emerging from the sea.

Their bodies lay flatly on the rocks, and their eyes regarded him with evil interest; but it does not appear that Mr. Fison was afraid, or that he realised that he was in any danger. Possibly his confidence is to be ascribed to the limpness of their attitudes. But he was horrified, of course, and intensely excited and indignant, at such revolting creatures preying upon human flesh. He thought they had chanced upon a drowned body. He shouted to them, with the idea of driving them off, and finding they did not budge, cast about him, picked up a big rounded lump of rock, and flung it at one.

And then, slowly uncoiling their tentacles, they all began moving towards him—creeping at first deliberately, and making a soft purring sound to each other.

In a moment Mr. Fison realised that he was in danger. He shouted again, threw both his boots, and started off, with a leap, forthwith. Twenty yards off he stopped and faced about, judging them slow, and behold! the tentacles of their leader were already pouring over the rocky ridge on which he had just been standing!

At that he shouted again, but this time not threatening, but a cry of dismay, and began jumping, striding, slipping, wading across the uneven expanse between him and the beach. The tall red cliffs seemed suddenly at a vast distance, and he saw, as though they were creatures in another world, two minute workmen engaged in the repair of the ladder-way, and little suspecting the race for life that was beginning below them. At one time he could hear the creatures splashing in the pools not a dozen feet behind him, and once he slipped and almost fell.

They chased him to the very foot of the cliffs, and desisted only when he had been joined by the workmen at the foot of the ladder-way up the cliff. All three of the men pelted them with stones for a time, and then hurried to the cliff top and along the path towards Sidmouth, to secure assistance and a boat, and to rescue the desecrated body from the clutches of these abominable creatures.

II.

And, as if he had not already been in sufficient peril that day, Mr. Fison went with the boat to point out the exact spot of his adventure.

As the tide was down, it required a considerable detour to reach the spot, and when at last they came off the ladder-way, the mangled body had disappeared. The water was now running in, submerging first one slab of slimy rock and then another, and the four men in the boat—the workmen, that is, the boatman, and Mr. Fison—now turned their attention from the bearings off shore to the water beneath the keel.

At first they could see little below them, save a dark jungle of laminaria, with an occasional darting fish. Their minds were set on adventure, and they expressed their disappointment freely. But presently they saw one of the monsters swimming through the water seaward, with a curious rolling motion that suggested to Mr. Fison the spinning roll of a captive balloon. Almost immediately after, the waving streamers of laminaria were extraordinarily perturbed, parted for a moment, and three of these beasts became darkly visible, struggling for what was probably some fragment of the drowned man. In a moment the copious olive-green ribbons had poured again over this writhing group.

At that all four men, greatly excited, began beating the water with oars and shouting, and immediately they saw a tumultuous movement among the weeds. They desisted to see more clearly, and as soon as the water was smooth, they saw, as it seemed to them, the whole sea bottom among the weeds set with eyes.

"Ugly swine!" cried one of the men. "Why, there's dozens!"

And forthwith the things began to rise through the water about them. Mr. Fison has since described to the writer this startling eruption out of the waving laminaria meadows. To him it seemed to occupy a considerable time, but it is probable that really it was an affair of a few seconds only. For a time nothing but eyes, and then he speaks of tentacles streaming out and parting the weed fronds this way and that. Then these things, growing larger, until at last the bottom was hidden by their intercoiling forms, and the tips of tentacles rose darkly here and there into the air above the swell of the waters.

One came up boldly to the side of the boat, and clinging to this with three of its sucker-set tentacles, threw four others over the gunwale, as if with an intention either of oversetting the boat or of clambering into it. Mr. Fison at once caught up the boat-hook, and, jabbing furiously at the soft tentacles, forced it to desist. He was struck in the back and almost pitched overboard by the boatman, who was using his oar to resist a similar attack on the other side of the boat. But the tentacles on either side at once relaxed their hold, slid out of sight, and splashed into the water.

"We'd better get out of this," said Mr. Fison, who was trembling violently. He went to the tiller, while the boatman and one of the workmen seated themselves and began rowing. The other workman stood up in the fore part of the boat, with the boat-hook, ready to strike any more tentacles that might appear. Nothing else seems to have been said. Mr. Fison had expressed the common feeling beyond amendment. In a hushed, scared mood, with faces white and drawn, they set about escaping from the position into which they had so recklessly blundered.

But the oars had scarcely dropped into the water before dark, tapering, serpentine ropes had bound them, and were about the rudder; and creeping up the sides of the boat with a looping motion came the suckers again. The men gripped their oars and pulled, but it was like trying to move a boat in a floating raft of weeds. "Help here!" cried the boatman, and Mr. Fison and the second workman rushed to help lug at the oar.

Then the man with the boat-hook—his name was Ewan, or Ewen—sprang up with a curse and began striking downward over the side, as far as he could reach, at the bank of tentacles that now clustered along the boat's bottom. And, at the same time, the two rowers stood up to get a better purchase for the recovery of their oars. The boatman handed his to Mr. Fison, who lugged desperately, and, meanwhile, the boatman opened a big clasp-knife, and leaning over the side of the boat, began hacking at the spiring arms upon the oar shaft.

Mr. Fison, staggering with the quivering rocking of the boat, his teeth set, his breath coming short, and the veins starting on his hands as he pulled at his oar, suddenly cast his eyes seaward. And there, not fifty yards off, across the long rollers of the incoming tide, was a large boat standing in towards them, with three women and a little child in it. A boatman was rowing, and a little man in a pink-ribboned straw hat and whites stood in the stern hailing them. For a moment, of course, Mr. Fison thought of help, and then he thought of the child. He abandoned his oar forthwith, threw up his arms in a frantic gesture, and screamed to the party in the boat to keep away "for God's sake!" It says much for the modesty and courage of Mr. Fison that he does not seem to be aware that there was any quality of heroism in his action at this juncture. The oar he had abandoned was at once drawn under, and presently reappeared floating about twenty yards away.

At the same moment Mr. Fison felt the boat under him lurch violently, and a hoarse scream, a prolonged cry of terror from Hill, the boatman, caused him to forget the party of excursionists altogether. He turned, and saw Hill crouching by the forward row-lock, his face convulsed with terror, and his right arm over the side and drawn tightly down. He gave now a succession of short, sharp cries, "Oh! oh! oh!—oh!" Mr. Fison believes that he must have been hacking at the tentacles below the water-line, and have been grasped by them, but, of course, it is quite impossible to say now certainly what had happened. The boat was heeling over, so that the gunwale was within ten inches of the water, and both Ewan and the other labourer were striking down into the water, with oar and boat-hook, on either side of Hill's arm. Mr. Fison instinctively placed himself to counterpoise them.

Then Hill, who was a burly, powerful man, made a strenuous effort, and rose almost to a standing position. He lifted his arm, indeed, clean out of the water. Hanging to it was a complicated tangle of brown ropes, and the eyes of one of the brutes that had hold of him, glaring straight and resolute, showed momentarily above the surface. The boat heeled more and more, and the green-brown water came pouring in a cascade over the side. Then Hill slipped and fell with his ribs across the side, and his arm and the mass of tentacles about it splashed back into the water. He rolled over; his boot kicked Mr. Fison's knee as that gentleman rushed forward to seize him, and in another moment fresh tentacles had whipped about his waist and neck, and after a brief, convulsive struggle, in which the boat was nearly capsized, Hill was lugged overboard. The boat righted with a violent jerk that all but sent Mr. Fison over the other side, and hid the struggle in the water from his eyes.

He stood staggering to recover his balance for a moment, and as he did so he became aware that the struggle and the inflowing tide had carried them close upon the weedy rocks again. Not four yards off a table of rock still rose in rhythmic movements above the in-wash of the tide. In a moment Mr. Fison seized the oar from Ewan, gave one vigorous stroke, then dropping it, ran to the bows and leapt. He felt his feet slide over the rock, and, by a frantic effort, leapt again towards a further mass. He stumbled over this, came to his knees, and rose again.

"Look out!" cried someone, and a large drab body struck him. He was knocked flat into a tidal pool by one of the workmen, and as he went down he heard smothered, choking cries, that he believed at the time came from Hill. Then he found himself marvelling at the shrillness and variety of Hill's voice. Someone jumped over him, and a curving rush of foamy water poured over him, and passed. He scrambled to his feet dripping, and without looking seaward, ran as fast as his terror would let him shoreward. Before him, over the flat space of scattered rocks, stumbled the two work-men—one a dozen yards in front of the other.

He looked over his shoulder at last, and seeing that he was not pursued, faced about. He was astonished. From the moment of the rising of the cephalopods out of the water he had been acting too swiftly to fully comprehend his actions. Now it seemed to him as if he had suddenly jumped out of an evil dream.

For there were the sky, cloudless and blazing with the afternoon sun, the sea weltering under its pitiless brightness, the soft creamy foam of the breaking water, and the low, long, dark ridges of rock. The righted boat floated, rising and falling gently on the swell about a dozen yards from shore. Hill and the monsters, all the stress and tumult of that fierce fight for life, had vanished as though they had never been.

Mr. Fison's heart was beating violently; he was throbbing to the finger-tips, and his breath came deep.

There was something missing. For some seconds he could not think clearly enough what this might be. Sun, sky, sea, rocks—what was it? Then he remembered the boat-load of excursionists. It had vanished. He wondered whether he had imagined it. He turned, and saw the two workmen standing side by side under the projecting masses of the tall pink cliffs. He hesitated whether he should make one last attempt to save the man Hill. His physical excitement seemed to desert him suddenly, and leave him aimless and helpless. He turned shoreward, stumbling and wading towards his two companions.

He looked back again, and there were now two boats floating, and the one farthest out at sea pitched clumsily, bottom upward.

III.

So it was Haploteuthis ferox made its appearance upon the Devonshire coast. So far, this has been its most serious aggression. Mr. Fison's account, taken together with the wave of boating and bathing casualties to which I have already alluded, and the absence of fish from the Cornish coasts that year, points clearly to a shoal of these voracious deep-sea monsters prowling slowly along the sub-tidal coast-line. Hunger migration has, I know, been suggested as the force that drove them hither; but, for my own part, I prefer to believe the alternative theory of Hemsley. Hemsley holds that a pack or shoal of these creatures may have become enamoured of human flesh by the accident of a foundered ship sinking among them, and have wandered in search of it out of their accustomed zone; first waylaying and following ships, and so coming to our shores in the wake of the Atlantic traffic. But to discuss Hemsley's cogent and admirably-stated arguments would be out of place here.

It would seem that the appetites of the shoal were satisfied by the catch of eleven people—for, so far as can be ascertained, there were ten people in the second boat, and certainly these creatures gave no further signs of their presence off Sidmouth that day. The coast between Seaton and Budleigh Salterton was patrolled all that evening and night by four Preventive Service boats, the men in which were armed with harpoons and cutlasses, and as the evening advanced, a number of more or less similarly equipped expeditions, organised by private individuals, joined them. Mr. Fison took no part in any of these expeditions.

About midnight excited hails were heard from a boat about a couple of miles out at sea to the south-east of Sidmouth, and a lantern was seen waving in a strange manner to and fro and up and down. The nearer boats at once hurried towards the alarm. The venturesome occupants of the boat—a seaman, a curate, and two schoolboys—had actually seen the monsters passing under their boat. The creatures, it seems, like most deep-sea organisms, were phosphorescent, and they had been floating, five fathoms deep or so, like creatures of moonshine through the blackness of the water, their tentacles retracted and as if asleep, rolling over and over, and moving slowly in a wedge-like formation towards the south-east.

These people told their story in gesticulated fragments, as first one boat drew alongside and then another. At last there was a little fleet of eight or nine boats collected together, and from them a tumult, like the chatter of a market-place, rose into the stillness of the night. There was little or no disposition to pursue the shoal, the people had neither weapons nor experience for such a dubious chase, and presently—even with a certain relief, it may be—the boats turned shoreward.

And now to tell what is perhaps the most astonishing fact in this whole astonishing raid. We have not the slightest knowledge of the subsequent movements of the shoal, although the whole south-west coast was now alert for it. But it may, perhaps, be significant that a cachalot was stranded off Sark on June 3. Two weeks and three days after this Sidmouth affair, a living Haploteuthis came ashore on Calais sands. It was alive, because several witnesses saw its tentacles moving in a convulsive way. But it is probable that it was dying. A gentleman named Pouchet obtained a rifle and shot it.

That was the last appearance of a living Haploteuthis. No others were seen on the French coast. On the 15th of June a dead carcass, almost complete, was washed ashore near Torquay, and a few days later a boat from the Marine Biological station, engaged in dredging off Plymouth, picked up a rotting specimen, slashed deeply with a cutlass wound. How the former had come by its death it is impossible to say. And on the last day of June, Mr. Egbert Caine, an artist, bathing near Newlyn, threw up his arms, shrieked, and was drawn under. A friend bathing with him made no attempt to save him, but swam at once for the shore. This is the last fact to tell of this extraordinary raid from the deeper sea. Whether it is really the last of these horrible creatures it is, as yet, premature to say. But it is believed, and certainly it is to be hoped, that they have returned now, and returned for good, to the sunless depths of the middle seas, out of which they have so strangely and so mysteriously arisen.

XIV.

THE OBLITERATED MAN.

I was—you shall hear immediately why I am not now—Egbert Craddock Cummins. The name remains. I am still (Heaven help me!) Dramatic Critic to the Fiery Cross. What I shall be in a little while I do not know. I write in great trouble and confusion of mind. I will do what I can to make myself clear in the face of terrible difficulties. You must bear with me a little. When a man is rapidly losing his own identity, he naturally finds a difficulty in expressing himself. I will make it perfectly plain in a minute, when once I get my grip upon the story. Let me see—where am I? I wish I knew. Ah, I have it! Dead self! Egbert Craddock Cummins!

In the past I should have disliked writing anything quite so full of "I" as this story must be. It is full of "I's" before and behind, like the beast in Revelation—the one with a head like a calf, I am afraid. But my tastes have changed since I became a Dramatic Critic and studied the masters—G.A.S., G.B.S., G.R.S., and the others. Everything has changed since then. At least the story is about myself—so that there is some excuse for me. And it is really not egotism, because, as I say, since those days my identity has undergone an entire alteration.

That past!... I was—in those days—rather a nice fellow, rather shy— taste for grey in my clothes, weedy little moustache, face "interesting," slight stutter which I had caught in my early life from a schoolfellow. Engaged to a very nice girl, named Delia. Fairly new, she was— cigarettes—liked me because I was human and original. Considered I was like Lamb—on the strength of the stutter, I believe. Father, an eminent authority on postage stamps. She read a great deal in the British Museum. (A perfect pairing ground for literary people, that British Museum—you should read George Egerton and Justin Huntly M'Carthy and Gissing and the rest of them.) We loved in our intellectual way, and shared the brightest hopes. (All gone now.) And her father liked me because I seemed honestly eager to hear about stamps. She had no mother. Indeed, I had the happiest prospects a young man could have. I never went to theatres in those days. My Aunt Charlotte before she died had told me not to.

Then Barnaby, the editor of the Fiery Cross, made me—in spite of my spasmodic efforts to escape—Dramatic Critic. He is a fine, healthy man, Barnaby, with an enormous head of frizzy black hair and a convincing manner, and he caught me on the staircase going to see Wembly. He had been dining, and was more than usually buoyant. "Hullo, Cummins!" he said. "The very man I want!" He caught me by the shoulder or the collar or something, ran me up the little passage, and flung me over the waste-paper basket into the arm-chair in his office. "Pray be seated," he said, as he did so. Then he ran across the room and came back with some pink and yellow tickets and pushed them into my hand. "Opera Comique," he said, "Thursday; Friday, the Surrey; Saturday, the Frivolity. That's all, I think."

"But—" I began.

"Glad you're free," he said, snatching some proofs off the desk and beginning to read.

"I don't quite understand," I said.

"Eigh?" he said, at the top of his voice, as though he thought I had gone and was startled at my remark.

"Do you want me to criticise these plays?"

"Do something with 'em... Did you think it was a treat?"

"But I can't."

"Did you call me a fool?"

"Well, I've never been to a theatre in my life."

"Virgin soil."

"But I don't know anything about it, you know."

"That's just it. New view. No habits. No clichés in stock. Ours is a live paper, not a bag of tricks. None of your clockwork professional journalism in this office. And I can rely on your integrity——"

"But I've conscientious scruples——"

He caught me up suddenly and put me outside his door. "Go and talk to

Wembly about that," he said. "He'll explain."

As I stood perplexed, he opened the door again, said, "I forgot this," thrust a fourth ticket into my hand (it was for that night—in twenty minutes' time) and slammed the door upon me. His expression was quite calm, but I caught his eye.

I hate arguments. I decided that I would take his hint and become (to my own destruction) a Dramatic Critic. I walked slowly down the passage to Wembly. That Barnaby has a remarkable persuasive way. He has made few suggestions during our very pleasant intercourse of four years that he has not ultimately won me round to adopting. It may be, of course, that I am of a yielding disposition; certainly I am too apt to take my colour from my circumstances. It is, indeed, to my unfortunate susceptibility to vivid impressions that all my misfortunes are due. I have already alluded to the slight stammer I had acquired from a schoolfellow in my youth. However, this is a digression... I went home in a cab to dress.

I will not trouble the reader with my thoughts about the first-night audience, strange assembly as it is,—those I reserve for my Memoirs,—nor the humiliating story of how I got lost during the entr'acte in a lot of red plush passages, and saw the third act from the gallery. The only point upon which I wish to lay stress was the remarkable effect of the acting upon me. You must remember I had lived a quiet and retired life, and had never been to the theatre before, and that I am extremely sensitive to vivid impressions. At the risk of repetition I must insist upon these points.

The first effect was a profound amazement, not untinctured by alarm. The phenomenal unnaturalness of acting is a thing discounted in the minds of most people by early visits to the theatre. They get used to the fantastic gestures, the flamboyant emotions, the weird mouthings, melodious snortings, agonising yelps, lip-gnawings, glaring horrors, and other emotional symbolism of the stage. It becomes at last a mere deaf-and-dumb language to them, which they read intelligently pari passu with the hearing of the dialogue. But all this was new to me. The thing was called a modern comedy, the people were supposed to be English and were dressed like fashionable Americans of the current epoch, and I fell into the natural error of supposing that the actors were trying to represent human beings. I looked round on my first-night audience with a kind of wonder, discovered—as all new Dramatic Critics do—that it rested with me to reform the Drama, and, after a supper choked with emotion, went off to the office to write a column, piebald with "new paragraphs" (as all my stuff is—it fills out so) and purple with indignation. Barnaby was delighted.

But I could not sleep that night. I dreamt of actors—actors glaring, actors smiting their chests, actors flinging out a handful of extended fingers, actors smiling bitterly, laughing despairingly, falling hopelessly, dying idiotically. I got up at eleven with a slight headache, read my notice in the Fiery Cross, breakfasted, and went back to my room to shave, (It's my habit to do so.) Then an odd thing happened. I could not find my razor. Suddenly it occurred to me that I had not unpacked it the day before.

"Ah!" said I, in front of the looking-glass. Then "Hullo!"

Quite involuntarily, when I had thought of my portmanteau, I had flung up the left arm (fingers fully extended) and clutched at my diaphragm with my right hand. I am an acutely self-conscious man at all times. The gesture struck me as absolutely novel for me. I repeated it, for my own satisfaction. "Odd!" Then (rather puzzled) I turned to my portmanteau.

After shaving, my mind reverted to the acting I had seen, and I entertained myself before the cheval glass with some imitations of Jafferay's more exaggerated gestures. "Really, one might think it a disease," I said—"Stage-Walkitis!" (There's many a truth spoken in jest.) Then, if I remember rightly, I went off to see Wembly, and afterwards lunched at the British Museum with Delia. We actually spoke about our prospects, in the light of my new appointment.

But that appointment was the beginning of my downfall. From that day I necessarily became a persistent theatre-goer, and almost insensibly I began to change. The next thing I noticed after the gesture about the razor was to catch myself bowing ineffably when I met Delia, and stooping in an old-fashioned, courtly way over her hand. Directly I caught myself, I straightened myself up and became very uncomfortable. I remember she looked at me curiously. Then, in the office, I found myself doing "nervous business," fingers on teeth, when Barnaby asked me a question I could not very well answer. Then, in some trifling difference with Delia, I clasped my hand to my brow. And I pranced through my social transactions at times singularly like an actor! I tried not to—no one could be more keenly alive to the arrant absurdity of the histrionic bearing. And I did!

It began to dawn on me what it all meant. The acting, I saw, was too much for my delicately-strung nervous system. I have always, I know, been too amenable to the suggestions of my circumstances. Night after night of concentrated attention to the conventional attitudes and intonation of the English stage was gradually affecting my speech and carriage. I was giving way to the infection of sympathetic imitation. Night after night my plastic nervous system took the print of some new amazing gesture, some new emotional exaggeration—and retained it. A kind of theatrical veneer threatened to plate over and obliterate my private individuality altogether. I saw myself in a kind of vision. Sitting by myself one night, my new self seemed to me to glide, posing and gesticulating, across the room. He clutched his throat, he opened his fingers, he opened his legs in walking like a high-class marionette. He went from attitude to attitude. He might have been clockwork. Directly after this I made an ineffectual attempt to resign my theatrical work. But Barnaby persisted in talking about the Polywhiddle Divorce all the time I was with him, and I could get no opportunity of saying what I wished.

And then Delia's manner began to change towards me. The ease of our intercourse vanished. I felt she was learning to dislike me. I grinned, and capered, and scowled, and posed at her in a thousand ways, and knew—with what a voiceless agony!—that I did it all the time. I tried to resign again, and Barnaby talked about "X" and "Z" and "Y" in the New Review, and gave me a strong cigar to smoke, and so routed me. And then I walked up the Assyrian Gallery in the manner of Irving to meet Delia, and so precipitated the crisis.

"Ah!—Dear!" I said, with more sprightliness and emotion in my voice than had ever been in all my life before I became (to my own undoing) a Dramatic Critic.

She held out her hand rather coldly, scrutinising my face as she did so. I prepared, with a new-won grace, to walk by her side. "Egbert," she said, standing still, and thought. Then she looked at me.

I said nothing. I felt what was coming. I tried to be the old Egbert Craddock Cummins of shambling gait and stammering sincerity, whom she loved, but I felt even as I did so that I was a new thing, a thing of surging emotions and mysterious fixity—like no human being that ever lived, except upon the stage. "Egbert," she said, "you are not yourself."

"Ah!" Involuntarily I clutched my diaphragm and averted my head (as is the way with them).

"There!" she said.

"What do you mean?" I said, whispering in vocal italics—you know how they do it—turning on her, perplexity on face, right hand down, left on brow. I knew quite well what she meant. I knew quite well the dramatic unreality of my behaviour. But I struggled against it in vain. "What do you mean?" I said, and, in a kind of hoarse whisper, "I don't understand!"

She really looked as though she disliked me. "What do you keep on posing for?" she said. "I don't like it. You didn't use to."

"Didn't use to!" I said slowly, repeating this twice. I glared up and down the gallery with short, sharp glances. "We are alone," I said swiftly. "Listen!" I poked my forefinger towards her, and glared at her. "I am under a curse."

I saw her hand tighten upon her sunshade. "You are under some bad influence or other," said Delia. "You should give it up. I never knew anyone change as you have done."

"Delia!" I said, lapsing into the pathetic. "Pity me, Augh! Delia! Pit—y me!"

She eyed me critically. "Why you keep playing the fool like this I don't know," she said. "Anyhow, I really cannot go about with a man who behaves as you do. You made us both ridiculous on Wednesday. Frankly, I dislike you, as you are now. I met you here to tell you so—as it's about the only place where we can be sure of being alone together——"

"Delia!" said I, with intensity, knuckles of clenched hands white. "You don't mean——"

"I do," said Delia. "A woman's lot is sad enough at the best of times. But with you——"

I clapped my hand on my brow.

"So, good-bye," said Delia, without emotion.

"Oh, Delia!" I said. "Not this?"

"Good-bye, Mr. Cummins," she said.

By a violent effort I controlled myself and touched her hand. I tried to say some word of explanation to her. She looked into my working face and winced. "I must do it," she said hopelessly. Then she turned from me and began walking rapidly down the gallery.

Heavens! How the human agony cried within me! I loved Delia. But nothing found expression—I was already too deeply crusted with my acquired self.

"Good-baye!" I said at last, watching her retreating figure. How I hated myself for doing it! After she had vanished, I repeated in a dreamy way, "Good-baye!" looking hopelessly round me. Then, with a kind of heart-broken cry, I shook my clenched fists in the air, staggered to the pedestal of a winged figure, buried my face in my arms, and made my shoulders heave. Something within me said "Ass!" as I did so. (I had the greatest difficulty in persuading the Museum policeman, who was attracted by my cry of agony, that I was not intoxicated, but merely suffering from a transient indisposition.)

But even this great sorrow has not availed to save me from my fate. I see it; everyone sees it: I grow more "theatrical" every day. And no one could be more painfully aware of the pungent silliness of theatrical ways. The quiet, nervous, but pleasing E.C. Cummins vanishes. I cannot save him. I am driven like a dead leaf before the winds of March. My tailor even enters into the spirit of my disorder. He has a peculiar sense of what is fitting. I tried to get a dull grey suit from him this spring, and he foisted a brilliant blue upon me, and I see he has put braid down the sides of my new dress trousers. My hairdresser insists upon giving me a "wave."

I am beginning to associate with actors. I detest them, but it is only in their company that I can feel I am not glaringly conspicuous. Their talk infects me. I notice a growing tendency to dramatic brevity, to dashes and pauses in my style, to a punctuation of bows and attitudes. Barnaby has remarked it too. I offended Wembly by calling him "Dear Boy" yesterday. I dread the end, but I cannot escape from it.

The fact is, I am being obliterated. Living a grey, retired life all my youth, I came to the theatre a delicate sketch of a man, a thing of tints and faint lines. Their gorgeous colouring has effaced me altogether. People forget how much mode of expression, method of movement, are a matter of contagion. I have heard of stage-struck people before, and thought it a figure of speech. I spoke of it jestingly, as a disease. It is no jest. It is a disease. And I have got it badly! Deep down within me I protest against the wrong done to my personality—unavailingly. For three hours or more a week I have to go and concentrate my attention on some fresh play, and the suggestions of the drama strengthen their awful hold upon me. My manners grow so flamboyant, my passions so professional, that I doubt, as I said at the outset, whether it is really myself that behaves in such a manner. I feel merely the core to this dramatic casing, that grows thicker and presses upon me—me and mine. I feel like King John's abbot in his cope of lead.

I doubt, indeed, whether I should not abandon the struggle altogether— leave this sad world of ordinary life for which I am so ill fitted, abandon the name of Cummins for some professional pseudonym, complete my self-effacement, and—a thing of tricks and tatters, of posing and pretence—go upon the stage. It seems my only resort—"to hold the mirror up to Nature." For in the ordinary life, I will confess, no one now seems to regard me as both sane and sober. Only upon the stage, I feel convinced, will people take me seriously. That will be the end of it. I know that will be the end of it. And yet ... I will frankly confess ... all that marks off your actor from your common man ... I detest. I am still largely of my Aunt Charlotte's opinion, that play-acting is unworthy of a pure-minded man's attention, much more participation. Even now I would resign my dramatic criticism and try a rest. Only I can't get hold of Barnaby. Letters of resignation he never notices. He says it is against the etiquette of journalism to write to your Editor. And when I go to see him, he gives me another big cigar and some strong whisky and soda, and then something always turns up to prevent my explanation.

XV.

THE PLATTNER STORY.

Whether the story of Gottfried Plattner is to be credited or not is a pretty question in the value of evidence. On the one hand, we have seven witnesses—to be perfectly exact, we have six and a half pairs of eyes, and one undeniable fact; and on the other we have—what is it?—prejudice, common-sense, the inertia of opinion. Never were there seven more honest-seeming witnesses; never was there a more undeniable fact than the inversion of Gottfried Plattner's anatomical structure, and—never was there a more preposterous story than the one they have to tell! The most preposterous part of the story is the worthy Gottfried's contribution (for I count him as one of the seven). Heaven forbid that I should be led into giving countenance to superstition by a passion for impartiality, and so come to share the fate of Eusapia's patrons! Frankly, I believe there is something crooked about this business of Gottfried Plattner; but what that crooked factor is, I will admit as frankly, I do not know. I have been surprised at the credit accorded to the story in the most unexpected and authoritative quarters. The fairest way to the reader, however, will be for me to tell it without further comment.

Gottfried Plattner is, in spite of his name, a freeborn Englishman. His father was an Alsatian who came to England in the 'sixties, married a respectable English girl of unexceptionable antecedents, and died, after a wholesome and uneventful life (devoted, I understand, chiefly to the laying of parquet flooring), in 1887. Gottfried's age is seven-and-twenty. He is, by virtue of his heritage of three languages, Modern Languages Master in a small private school in the south of England. To the casual observer he is singularly like any other Modern Languages Master in any other small private school. His costume is neither very costly nor very fashionable, but, on the other hand, it is not markedly cheap or shabby; his complexion, like his height and his bearing, is inconspicuous. You would notice, perhaps, that, like the majority of people, his face was not absolutely symmetrical, his right eye a little larger than the left, and his jaw a trifle heavier on the right side. If you, as an ordinary careless person, were to bare his chest and feel his heart beating, you would probably find it quite like the heart of anyone else. But here you and the trained observer would part company. If you found his heart quite ordinary, the trained observer would find it quite otherwise. And once the thing was pointed out to you, you too would perceive the peculiarity easily enough. It is that Gottfried's heart beats on the right side of his body.

Now, that is not the only singularity of Gottfried's structure, although it is the only one that would appeal to the untrained mind. Careful sounding of Gottfried's internal arrangements by a well-known surgeon seems to point to the fact that all the other unsymmetrical parts of his body are similarly misplaced. The right lobe of his liver is on the left side, the left on his right; while his lungs, too, are similarly contraposed. What is still more singular, unless Gottfried is a consummate actor, we must believe that his right hand has recently become his left. Since the occurrences we are about to consider (as impartially as possible), he has found the utmost difficulty in writing, except from right to left across the paper with his left hand. He cannot throw with his right hand, he is perplexed at meal-times between knife and fork, and his ideas of the rule of the road—he is a cyclist—are still a dangerous confusion. And there is not a scrap of evidence to show that before these occurrences Gottfried was at all left-handed.

There is yet another wonderful fact in this preposterous business. Gottfried produces three photographs of himself. You have him at the age of five or six, thrusting fat legs at you from under a plaid frock, and scowling. In that photograph his left eye is a little larger than his right, and his jaw is a trifle heavier on the left side. This is the reverse of his present living condition. The photograph of Gottfried at fourteen seems to contradict these facts, but that is because it is one of those cheap "Gem" photographs that were then in vogue, taken direct upon metal, and therefore reversing things just as a looking-glass would. The third photograph represents him at one-and-twenty, and confirms the record of the others. There seems here evidence of the strongest confirmatory character that Gottfried has exchanged his left side for his right. Yet how a human being can be so changed, short of a fantastic and pointless miracle, it is exceedingly hard to suggest.

In one way, of course, these facts might be explicable on the supposition that Plattner has undertaken an elaborate mystification, on the strength of his heart's displacement. Photographs may be faked, and left-handedness imitated. But the character of the man does not lend itself to any such theory. He is quiet, practical, unobtrusive, and thoroughly sane, from the Nordau standpoint. He likes beer, and smokes moderately, takes walking exercise daily, and has a healthily high estimate of the value of his teaching. He has a good but untrained tenor voice, and takes a pleasure in singing airs of a popular and cheerful character. He is fond, but not morbidly fond, of reading,—chiefly fiction pervaded with a vaguely pious optimism,—sleeps well, and rarely dreams. He is, in fact, the very last person to evolve a fantastic fable. Indeed, so far from forcing this story upon the world, he has been singularly reticent on the matter. He meets enquirers with a certain engaging—bashfulness is almost the word, that disarms the most suspicious. He seems genuinely ashamed that anything so unusual has occurred to him.

It is to be regretted that Plattner's aversion to the idea of post-mortem dissection may postpone, perhaps for ever, the positive proof that his entire body has had its left and right sides transposed. Upon that fact mainly the credibility of his story hangs. There is no way of taking a man and moving him about in space as ordinary people understand space, that will result in our changing his sides. Whatever you do, his right is still his right, his left his left. You can do that with a perfectly thin and flat thing, of course. If you were to cut a figure out of paper, any figure with a right and left side, you could change its sides simply by lifting it up and turning it over. But with a solid it is different. Mathematical theorists tell us that the only way in which the right and left sides of a solid body can be changed is by taking that body clean out of space as we know it,—taking it out of ordinary existence, that is, and turning it somewhere outside space. This is a little abstruse, no doubt, but anyone with any knowledge of mathematical theory will assure the reader of its truth. To put the thing in technical language, the curious inversion of Plattner's right and left sides is proof that he has moved out of our space into what is called the Fourth Dimension, and that he has returned again to our world. Unless we choose to consider ourselves the victims of an elaborate and motiveless fabrication, we are almost bound to believe that this has occurred.

So much for the tangible facts. We come now to the account of the phenomena that attended his temporary disappearance from the world. It appears that in the Sussexville Proprietary School, Plattner not only discharged the duties of Modern Languages Master, but also taught chemistry, commercial geography, bookkeeping, shorthand, drawing, and any other additional subject to which the changing fancies of the boys' parents might direct attention. He knew little or nothing of these various subjects, but in secondary as distinguished from Board or elementary schools, knowledge in the teacher is, very properly, by no means so necessary as high moral character and gentlemanly tone. In chemistry he was particularly deficient, knowing, he says, nothing beyond the Three Gases (whatever the three gases may be). As, however, his pupils began by knowing nothing, and derived all their information from him, this caused him (or anyone) but little inconvenience for several terms. Then a little boy named Whibble joined the school, who had been educated (it seems) by some mischievous relative into an inquiring habit of mind. This little boy followed Plattner's lessons with marked and sustained interest, and in order to exhibit his zeal on the subject, brought, at various times, substances for Plattner to analyse. Plattner, flattered by this evidence of his power of awakening interest, and trusting to the boy's ignorance, analysed these, and even, made general statements as to their composition. Indeed, he was so far stimulated by his pupil as to obtain a work upon analytical chemistry, and study it during his supervision of the evening's preparation. He was surprised to find chemistry quite an interesting subject.

So far the story is absolutely commonplace. But now the greenish powder comes upon the scene. The source of that greenish powder seems, unfortunately, lost. Master Whibble tells a tortuous story of finding it done up in a packet in a disused limekiln near the Downs. It would have been an excellent thing for Plattner, and possibly for Master Whibble's family, if a match could have been applied to that powder there and then. The young gentleman certainly did not bring it to school in a packet, but in a common eight-ounce graduated medicine bottle, plugged with masticated newspaper. He gave it to Plattner at the end of the afternoon school. Four boys had been detained after school prayers in order to complete some neglected tasks, and Plattner was supervising these in the small class-room in which the chemical teaching was conducted. The appliances for the practical teaching of chemistry in the Sussexville Proprietary School, as in most small schools in this country, are characterised by a severe simplicity. They are kept in a small cupboard standing in a recess, and having about the same capacity as a common travelling trunk. Plattner, being bored with his passive superintendence, seems to have welcomed the intervention of Whibble with his green powder as an agreeable diversion, and, unlocking this cupboard, proceeded at once with his analytical experiments. Whibble sat, luckily for himself, at a safe distance, regarding him. The four malefactors, feigning a profound absorption in their work, watched him furtively with the keenest interest. For even within the limits of the Three Gases, Plattner's practical chemistry was, I understand, temerarious.

They are practically unanimous in their account of Plattner's proceedings. He poured a little of the green powder into a test-tube, and tried the substance with water, hydrochloric acid, nitric acid, and sulphuric acid in succession. Getting no result, he emptied out a little heap—nearly half the bottleful, in fact—upon a slate and tried a match. He held the medicine bottle in his left hand. The stuff began to smoke and melt, and then exploded with deafening violence and a blinding flash.

The five boys, seeing the flash and being prepared for catastrophes, ducked below their desks, and were none of them seriously hurt. The window was blown out into the playground, and the blackboard on its easel was upset. The slate was smashed to atoms. Some plaster fell from the ceiling. No other damage was done to the school edifice or appliances, and the boys at first, seeing nothing of Plattner, fancied he was knocked down and lying out of their sight below the desks. They jumped out of their places to go to his assistance, and were amazed to find the space empty. Being still confused by the sudden violence of the report, they hurried to the open door, under the impression that he must have been hurt, and have rushed out of the room. But Carson, the foremost, nearly collided in the doorway with the principal, Mr. Lidgett.

Mr. Lidgett is a corpulent, excitable man with one eye. The boys describe him as stumbling into the room mouthing some of those tempered expletives irritable schoolmasters accustom themselves to use—lest worse befall. "Wretched mumchancer!" he said. "Where's Mr. Plattner?" The boys are agreed on the very words. ("Wobbler," "snivelling puppy," and "mumchancer" are, it seems, among the ordinary small change of Mr. Lidgett's scholastic commerce.)

Where's Mr. Plattner? That was a question that was to be repeated many times in the next few days. It really seemed as though that frantic hyperbole, "blown to atoms," had for once realised itself. There was not a visible particle of Plattner to be seen; not a drop of blood nor a stitch of clothing to be found. Apparently he had been blown clean out of existence and left not a wrack behind. Not so much as would cover a sixpenny piece, to quote a proverbial expression! The evidence of his absolute disappearance as a consequence of that explosion is indubitable.

It is not necessary to enlarge here upon the commotion excited in the Sussexville Proprietary School, and in Sussexville and elsewhere, by this event. It is quite possible, indeed, that some of the readers of these pages may recall the hearing of some remote and dying version of that excitement during the last summer holidays. Lidgett, it would seem, did everything in his power to suppress and minimise the story. He instituted a penalty of twenty-five lines for any mention of Plattner's name among the boys, and stated in the schoolroom that he was clearly aware of his assistant's whereabouts. He was afraid, he explains, that the possibility of an explosion happening, in spite of the elaborate precautions taken to minimise the practical teaching of chemistry, might injure the reputation of the school; and so might any mysterious quality in Plattner's departure. Indeed, he did everything in his power to make the occurrence seem as ordinary as possible. In particular, he cross-examined the five eye-witnesses of the occurrence so searchingly that they began to doubt the plain evidence of their senses. But, in spite of these efforts, the tale, in a magnified and distorted state, made a nine days' wonder in the district, and several parents withdrew their sons on colourable pretexts. Not the least remarkable point in the matter is the fact that a large number of people in the neighbourhood dreamed singularly vivid dreams of Plattner during the period of excitement before his return, and that these dreams had a curious uniformity. In almost all of them Plattner was seen, sometimes singly, sometimes in company, wandering about through a coruscating iridescence. In all cases his face was pale and distressed, and in some he gesticulated towards the dreamer. One or two of the boys, evidently under the influence of nightmare, fancied that Plattner approached them with remarkable swiftness, and seemed to look closely into their very eyes. Others fled with Plattner from the pursuit of vague and extraordinary creatures of a globular shape. But all these fancies were forgotten in inquiries and speculations when on the Wednesday next but one after the Monday of the explosion, Plattner returned.

The circumstances of his return were as singular as those of his departure. So far as Mr. Lidgett's somewhat choleric outline can be filled in from Plattner's hesitating statements, it would appear that on Wednesday evening, towards the hour of sunset, the former gentleman, having dismissed evening preparation, was engaged in his garden, picking and eating strawberries, a fruit of which he is inordinately fond. It is a large old-fashioned garden, secured from observation, fortunately, by a high and ivy-covered red-brick wall. Just as he was stooping over a particularly prolific plant, there was a flash in the air and a heavy thud, and before he could look round, some heavy body struck him violently from behind. He was pitched forward, crushing the strawberries he held in his hand, and that so roughly, that his silk hat—Mr. Lidgett adheres to the older ideas of scholastic costume—was driven violently down upon his forehead, and almost over one eye. This heavy missile, which slid over him sideways and collapsed into a sitting posture among the strawberry plants, proved to be our long-lost Mr. Gottfried Plattner, in an extremely dishevelled condition. He was collarless and hatless, his linen was dirty, and there was blood upon his hands. Mr. Lidgett was so indignant and surprised that he remained on all-fours, and with his hat jammed down on his eye, while he expostulated vehemently with Plattner for his disrespectful and unaccountable conduct.

This scarcely idyllic scene completes what I may call the exterior version of the Plattner story—its exoteric aspect. It is quite unnecessary to enter here into all the details of his dismissal by Mr. Lidgett. Such details, with the full names and dates and references, will be found in the larger report of these occurrences that was laid before the Society for the Investigation of Abnormal Phenomena. The singular transposition of Plattner's right and left sides was scarcely observed for the first day or so, and then first in connection with his disposition to write from right to left across the blackboard. He concealed rather than ostended this curious confirmatory circumstance, as he considered it would unfavourably affect his prospects in a new situation. The displacement of his heart was discovered some months after, when he was having a tooth extracted under anaesthetics. He then, very unwillingly, allowed a cursory surgical examination to be made of himself, with a view to a brief account in the Journal of Anatomy. That exhausts the statement of the material facts; and we may now go on to consider Plattner's account of the matter.

But first let us clearly differentiate between the preceding portion of this story and what is to follow. All I have told thus far is established by such evidence as even a criminal lawyer would approve. Every one of the witnesses is still alive; the reader, if he have the leisure, may hunt the lads out to-morrow, or even brave the terrors of the redoubtable Lidgett, and cross-examine and trap and test to his heart's content; Gottfried Plattner himself, and his twisted heart and his three photographs, are producible. It may be taken as proved that he did disappear for nine days as the consequence of an explosion; that he returned almost as violently, under circumstances in their nature annoying to Mr. Lidgett, whatever the details of those circumstances may be; and that he returned inverted, just as a reflection returns from a mirror. From the last fact, as I have already stated, it follows almost inevitably that Plattner, during those nine days, must have been in some state of existence altogether out of space. The evidence to these statements is, indeed, far stronger than that upon which most murderers are hanged. But for his own particular account of where he had been, with its confused explanations and wellnigh self-contradictory details, we have only Mr. Gottfried Plattner's word. I do not wish to discredit that, but I must point out—what so many writers upon obscure psychic phenomena fail to do—that we are passing here from the practically undeniable to that kind of matter which any reasonable man is entitled to believe or reject as he thinks proper. The previous statements render it plausible; its discordance with common experience tilts it towards the incredible. I would prefer not to sway the beam of the reader's judgment either way, but simply to tell the story as Plattner told it me.

He gave me his narrative, I may state, at my house at Chislehurst, and so soon as he had left me that evening, I went into my study and wrote down everything as I remembered it. Subsequently he was good enough to read over a type-written copy, so that its substantial correctness is undeniable.

He states that at the moment of the explosion he distinctly thought he was killed. He felt lifted off his feet and driven forcibly backward. It is a curious fact for psychologists that he thought clearly during his backward flight, and wondered whether he should hit the chemistry cupboard or the blackboard easel. His heels struck ground, and he staggered and fell heavily into a sitting position on something soft and firm. For a moment the concussion stunned him. He became aware at once of a vivid scent of singed hair, and he seemed to hear the voice of Lidgett asking for him. You will understand that for a time his mind was greatly confused.

At first he was under the impression that he was still standing in the class-room. He perceived quite distinctly the surprise of the boys and the entry of Mr. Lidgett. He is quite positive upon that score. He did not hear their remarks; but that he ascribed to the deafening effect of the experiment. Things about him seemed curiously dark and faint, but his mind explained that on the obvious but mistaken idea that the explosion had engendered a huge volume of dark smoke. Through the dimness the figures of Lidgett and the boys moved, as faint and silent as ghosts. Plattner's face still tingled with the stinging heat of the flash. He, was, he says, "all muddled." His first definite thoughts seem to have been of his personal safety. He thought he was perhaps blinded and deafened. He felt his limbs and face in a gingerly manner. Then his perceptions grew clearer, and he was astonished to miss the old familiar desks and other schoolroom furniture about him. Only dim, uncertain, grey shapes stood in the place of these. Then came a thing that made him shout aloud, and awoke his stunned faculties to instant activity. Two of the boys, gesticulating, walked one after the other clean through him! Neither manifested the slightest consciousness of his presence. It is difficult to imagine the sensation he felt. They came against him, he says, with no more force than a wisp of mist.

Plattner's first thought after that was that he was dead. Having been brought up with thoroughly sound views in these matters, however, he was a little surprised to find his body still about him. His second conclusion was that he was not dead, but that the others were: that the explosion had destroyed the Sussexville Proprietary School and every soul in it except himself. But that, too, was scarcely satisfactory. He was thrown back upon astonished observation.

Everything about him was profoundly dark: at first it seemed to have an altogether ebony blackness. Overhead was a black firmament. The only touch of light in the scene was a faint greenish glow at the edge of the sky in one direction, which threw into prominence a horizon of undulating black hills. This, I say, was his impression at first. As his eye grew accustomed to the darkness, he began to distinguish a faint quality of differentiating greenish colour in the circumambient night. Against this background the furniture and occupants of the class-room, it seems, stood out like phosphorescent spectres, faint and impalpable. He extended his hand, and thrust it without an effort through the wall of the room by the fireplace.

He describes himself as making a strenuous effort to attract attention. He shouted to Lidgett, and tried to seize the boys as they went to and fro. He only desisted from these attempts when Mrs. Lidgett, whom he (as an Assistant Master) naturally disliked, entered the room. He says the sensation of being in the world, and yet not a part of it, was an extraordinarily disagreeable one. He compared his feelings, not inaptly, to those of a cat watching a mouse through a window. Whenever he made a motion to communicate with the dim, familiar world about him, he found an invisible, incomprehensible barrier preventing intercourse.

He then turned his attention to his solid environment. He found the medicine bottle still unbroken in his hand, with the remainder of the green powder therein. He put this in his pocket, and began to feel about him. Apparently he was sitting on a boulder of rock covered with a velvety moss. The dark country about him he was unable to see, the faint, misty picture of the schoolroom blotting it out, but he had a feeling (due perhaps to a cold wind) that he was near the crest of a hill, and that a steep valley fell away beneath his feet. The green glow along the edge of the sky seemed to be growing in extent and intensity. He stood up, rubbing his eyes.

It would seem that he made a few steps, going steeply downhill, and then stumbled, nearly fell, and sat down again upon a jagged mass of rock to watch the dawn. He became aware that the world about him was absolutely silent. It was as still as it was dark, and though there was a cold wind blowing up the hill-face, the rustle of grass, the soughing of the boughs that should have accompanied it, were absent. He could hear, therefore, if he could not see, that the hillside upon which he stood was rocky and desolate. The green grew brighter every moment, and as it did so a faint, transparent blood-red mingled with, but did not mitigate, the blackness of the sky overhead and the rocky desolations about him. Having regard to what follows, I am inclined to think that that redness may have been an optical effect due to contrast. Something black fluttered momentarily against the livid yellow-green of the lower sky, and then the thin and penetrating voice of a bell rose out of the black gulf below him. An oppressive expectation grew with the growing light.

It is probable that an hour or more elapsed while he sat there, the strange green light growing brighter every moment, and spreading slowly, in flamboyant fingers, upward towards the zenith. As it grew, the spectral vision of our world became relatively or absolutely fainter. Probably both, for the time must have been about that of our earthly sunset. So far as his vision of our world went, Plattner, by his few steps downhill, had passed through the floor of the class-room, and was now, it seemed, sitting in mid-air in the larger schoolroom downstairs. He saw the boarders distinctly, but much more faintly than he had seen Lidgett. They were preparing their evening tasks, and he noticed with interest that several were cheating with their Euclid riders by means of a crib, a compilation whose existence he had hitherto never suspected. As the time passed, they faded steadily, as steadily as the light of the green dawn increased.

Looking down into the valley, he saw that the light had crept far down its rocky sides, and that the profound blackness of the abyss was now broken by a minute green glow, like the light of a glow-worm. And almost immediately the limb of a huge heavenly body of blazing green rose over the basaltic undulations of the distant hills, and the monstrous hill-masses about him came out gaunt and desolate, in green light and deep, ruddy black shadows. He became aware of a vast number of ball-shaped objects drifting as thistledown drifts over the high ground. There were none of these nearer to him than the opposite side of the gorge. The bell below twanged quicker and quicker, with something like impatient insistence, and several lights moved hither and thither. The boys at work at their desks were now almost imperceptibly faint.

This extinction of our world, when the green sun of this other universe rose, is a curious point upon which Plattner insists. During the Other-World night it is difficult to move about, on account of the vividness with which the things of this world are visible. It becomes a riddle to explain why, if this is the case, we in this world catch no glimpse of the Other-World. It is due, perhaps, to the comparatively vivid illumination of this world of ours. Plattner describes the midday of the Other-World, at its brightest, as not being nearly so bright as this world at full moon, while its night is profoundly black. Consequently, the amount of light, even in an ordinary dark room, is sufficient to render the things of the Other-World invisible, on the same principle that faint phosphorescence is only visible in the profoundest darkness. I have tried, since he told me his story, to see something of the Other-World by sitting for a long space in a photographer's dark room at night. I have certainly seen indistinctly the form of greenish slopes and rocks, but only, I must admit, very indistinctly indeed. The reader may possibly be more successful. Plattner tells me that since his return he has dreamt and seen and recognised places in the Other-World, but this is probably due to his memory of these scenes. It seems quite possible that people with unusually keen eyesight may occasionally catch a glimpse of this strange Other-World about us.

However, this is a digression. As the green sun rose, a long street of black buildings became perceptible, though only darkly and indistinctly, in the gorge, and after some hesitation, Plattner began to clamber down the precipitous descent towards them. The descent was long and exceedingly tedious, being so not only by the extraordinary steepness, but also by reason of the looseness of the boulders with which the whole face of the hill was strewn. The noise of his descent—now and then his heels struck fire from the rocks—seemed now the only sound in the universe, for the beating of the bell had ceased. As he drew nearer, he perceived that the various edifices had a singular resemblance to tombs and mausoleums and monuments, saving only that they were all uniformly black instead of being white, as most sepulchres are. And then he saw, crowding out of the largest building, very much as people disperse from church, a number of pallid, rounded, pale-green figures. These dispersed in several directions about the broad street of the place, some going through side alleys and reappearing upon the steepness of the hill, others entering some of the small black buildings which lined the way.

At the sight of these things drifting up towards him, Plattner stopped, staring. They were not walking, they were indeed limbless, and they had the appearance of human heads, beneath which a tadpole-like body swung. He was too astonished at their strangeness, too full, indeed, of strangeness, to be seriously alarmed by them. They drove towards him, in front of the chill wind that was blowing uphill, much as soap-bubbles drive before a draught. And as he looked at the nearest of those approaching, he saw it was indeed a human head, albeit with singularly large eyes, and wearing such an expression of distress and anguish as he had never seen before upon mortal countenance. He was surprised to find that it did not turn to regard him, but seemed to be watching and following some unseen moving thing. For a moment he was puzzled, and then it occurred to him that this creature was watching with its enormous eyes something that was happening in the world he had just left. Nearer it came, and nearer, and he was too astonished to cry out. It made a very faint fretting sound as it came close to him. Then it struck his face with a gentle pat—its touch was very cold—and drove past him, and upward towards the crest of the hill.

An extraordinary conviction flashed across Plattner's mind that this head had a strong likeness to Lidgett. Then he turned his attention to the other heads that were now swarming thickly up the hill-side. None made the slightest sign of recognition. One or two, indeed, came close to his head and almost followed the example of the first, but he dodged convulsively out of the way. Upon most of them he saw the same expression of unavailing regret he had seen upon the first, and heard the same faint sounds of wretchedness from them. One or two wept, and one rolling swiftly uphill wore an expression of diabolical rage. But others were cold, and several had a look of gratified interest in their eyes. One, at least, was almost in an ecstasy of happiness. Plattner does not remember that he recognised any more likenesses in those he saw at this time.

For several hours, perhaps, Plattner watched these strange things dispersing themselves over the hills, and not till long after they had ceased to issue from the clustering black buildings in the gorge, did he resume his downward climb. The darkness about him increased so much that he had a difficulty in stepping true. Overhead the sky was now a bright, pale green. He felt neither hunger nor thirst. Later, when he did, he found a chilly stream running down the centre of the gorge, and the rare moss upon the boulders, when he tried it at last in desperation, was good to eat.

He groped about among the tombs that ran down the gorge, seeking vaguely for some clue to these inexplicable things. After a long time he came to the entrance of the big mausoleum-like building from which the heads had issued. In this he found a group of green lights burning upon a kind of basaltic altar, and a bell-rope from a belfry overhead hanging down into the centre of the place. Round the wall ran a lettering of fire in a character unknown to him. While he was still wondering at the purport of these things, he heard the receding tramp of heavy feet echoing far down the street. He ran out into the darkness again, but he could see nothing. He had a mind to pull the bell-rope, and finally decided to follow the footsteps. But, although he ran far, he never overtook them; and his shouting was of no avail. The gorge seemed to extend an interminable distance. It was as dark as earthly starlight throughout its length, while the ghastly green day lay along the upper edge of its precipices. There were none of the heads, now, below. They were all, it seemed, busily occupied along the upper slopes. Looking up, he saw them drifting hither and thither, some hovering stationary, some flying swiftly through the air. It reminded him, he said, of "big snowflakes"; only these were black and pale green.

In pursuing the firm, undeviating footsteps that he never overtook, in groping into new regions of this endless devil's dyke, in clambering up and down the pitiless heights, in wandering about the summits, and in watching the drifting faces, Plattner states that he spent the better part of seven or eight days. He did not keep count, he says. Though once or twice he found eyes watching him, he had word with no living soul. He slept among the rocks on the hillside. In the gorge things earthly were invisible, because, from the earthly standpoint, it was far underground. On the altitudes, so soon as the earthly day began, the world became visible to him. He found himself sometimes stumbling over the dark green rocks, or arresting himself on a precipitous brink, while all about him the green branches of the Sussexville lanes were swaying; or, again, he seemed to be walking through the Sussexville streets, or watching unseen the private business of some household. And then it was he discovered, that to almost every human being in our world there pertained some of these drifting heads; that everyone in the world is watched intermittently by these helpless disembodiments.

What are they—these Watchers of the Living? Plattner never learned. But two, that presently found and followed him, were like his childhood's memory of his father and mother. Now and then other faces turned their eyes upon him: eyes like those of dead people who had swayed him, or injured him, or helped him in his youth and manhood. Whenever they looked at him, Plattner was overcome with a strange sense of responsibility. To his mother he ventured to speak; but she made no answer. She looked sadly, steadfastly, and tenderly—a little reproachfully, too, it seemed—into his eyes.

He simply tells this story: he does not endeavour to explain. We are left to surmise who these Watchers of the Living may be, or, if they are indeed the Dead, why they should so closely and passionately watch a world they have left for ever. It may be—indeed to my mind it seems just—that, when our life has closed, when evil or good is no longer a choice for us, we may still have to witness the working out of the train of consequences we have laid. If human souls continue after death, then surely human interests continue after death. But that is merely my own guess at the meaning of the things seen. Plattner offers no interpretation, for none was given him. It is well the reader should understand this clearly. Day after day, with his head reeling, he wandered about this strange lit world outside the world, weary and, towards the end, weak and hungry. By day—by our earthly day, that is—the ghostly vision of the old familiar scenery of Sussexville, all about him, irked and worried him. He could not see where to put his feet, and ever and again with a chilly touch one of these Watching Souls would come against his face. And after dark the multitude of these Watchers about him, and their intent distress, confused his mind beyond describing. A great longing to return to the earthly life that was so near and yet so remote consumed him. The unearthliness of things about him produced a positively painful mental distress. He was worried beyond describing by his own particular followers. He would shout at them to desist from staring at him, scold at them, hurry away from them. They were always mute and intent. Run as he might over the uneven ground, they followed his destinies.

On the ninth day, towards evening, Plattner heard the invisible footsteps approaching, far away down the gorge. He was then wandering over the broad crest of the same hill upon which he had fallen in his entry into this strange Other-World of his. He turned to hurry down into the gorge, feeling his way hastily, and was arrested by the sight of the thing that was happening in a room in a back street near the school. Both of the people in the room he knew by sight. The windows were open, the blinds up, and the setting sun shone clearly into it, so that it came out quite brightly at first, a vivid oblong of room, lying like a magic-lantern picture upon the black landscape and the livid green dawn. In addition to the sunlight, a candle had just been lit in the room.

On the bed lay a lank man, his ghastly white face terrible upon the tumbled pillow. His clenched hands were raised above his head. A little table beside the bed carried a few medicine bottles, some toast and water, and an empty glass. Every now and then the lank man's lips fell apart, to indicate a word he could not articulate. But the woman did not notice that he wanted anything, because she was busy turning out papers from an old-fashioned bureau in the opposite corner of the room. At first the picture was very vivid indeed, but as the green dawn behind it grew brighter and brighter, so it became fainter and more and more transparent.

As the echoing footsteps paced nearer and nearer, those footsteps that sound so loud in that Other-World and come so silently in this, Plattner perceived about him a great multitude of dim faces gathering together out of the darkness and watching the two people in the room. Never before had he seen so many of the Watchers of the Living. A multitude had eyes only for the sufferer in the room, another multitude, in infinite anguish, watched the woman as she hunted with greedy eyes for something she could not find. They crowded about Plattner, they came across his sight and buffeted his face, the noise of their unavailing regrets was all about him. He saw clearly only now and then. At other times the picture quivered dimly, through the veil of green reflections upon their movements. In the room it must have been very still, and Plattner says the candle flame streamed up into a perfectly vertical line of smoke, but in his ears each footfall and its echoes beat like a clap of thunder. And the faces! Two, more particularly near the woman's: one a woman's also, white and clear-featured, a face which might have once been cold and hard, but which was now softened by the touch of a wisdom strange to earth. The other might have been the woman's father. Both were evidently absorbed in the contemplation of some act of hateful meanness, so it seemed, which they could no longer guard against and prevent. Behind were others, teachers, it may be, who had taught ill, friends whose influence had failed. And over the man, too—a multitude, but none that seemed to be parents or teachers! Faces that might once have been coarse, now purged to strength by sorrow! And in the forefront one face, a girlish one, neither angry nor remorseful, but merely patient and weary, and, as it seemed to Plattner, waiting for relief. His powers of description fail him at the memory of this multitude of ghastly countenances. They gathered on the stroke of the bell. He saw them all in the space of a second. It would seem that he was so worked on by his excitement that, quite involuntarily, his restless fingers took the bottle of green powder out of his pocket and held it before him. But he does not remember that.

Abruptly the footsteps ceased. He waited for the next, and there was silence, and then suddenly, cutting through the unexpected stillness like a keen, thin blade, came the first stroke of the bell. At that the multitudinous faces swayed to and fro, and a louder crying began all about him. The woman did not hear; she was burning something now in the candle flame. At the second stroke everything grew dim, and a breath of wind, icy cold, blew through the host of watchers. They swirled about him like an eddy of dead leaves in the spring, and at the third stroke something was extended through them to the bed. You have heard of a beam of light. This was like a beam of darkness, and looking again at it, Plattner saw that it was a shadowy arm and hand.

The green sun was now topping the black desolations of the horizon, and the vision of the room was very faint. Plattner could see that the white of the bed struggled, and was convulsed; and that the woman looked round over her shoulder at it, startled.

The cloud of watchers lifted high like a puff of green dust before the wind, and swept swiftly downward towards the temple in the gorge. Then suddenly Plattner understood the meaning of the shadowy black arm that stretched across his shoulder and clutched its prey. He did not dare turn his head to see the Shadow behind the arm. With a violent effort, and covering his eyes, he set himself to run, made, perhaps, twenty strides, then slipped on a boulder, and fell. He fell forward on his hands; and the bottle smashed and exploded as he touched the ground.

In another moment he found himself, stunned and bleeding, sitting face to face with Lidgett in the old walled garden behind the school.

* * * * *

There the story of Plattner's experiences ends. I have resisted, I believe successfully, the natural disposition of a writer of fiction to dress up incidents of this sort. I have told the thing as far as possible in the order in which Plattner told it to me. I have carefully avoided any attempt at style, effect, or construction. It would have been easy, for instance, to have worked the scene of the death-bed into a kind of plot in which Plattner might have been involved. But, quite apart from the objectionableness of falsifying a most extraordinary true story, any such trite devices would spoil, to my mind, the peculiar effect of this dark world, with its livid green illumination and its drifting Watchers of the Living, which, unseen and unapproachable to us, is yet lying all about us.

It remains to add that a death did actually occur in Vincent Terrace, just beyond the school garden, and, so far as can be proved, at the moment of Plattner's return. Deceased was a rate-collector and insurance agent. His widow, who was much younger than himself, married last month a Mr. Whymper, a veterinary surgeon of Allbeeding. As the portion of this story given here has in various forms circulated orally in Sussexville, she has consented to my use of her name, on condition that I make it distinctly known that she emphatically contradicts every detail of Plattner's account of her husband's last moments. She burnt no will, she says, although Plattner never accused her of doing so; her husband made but one will, and that just after their marriage. Certainly, from a man who had never seen it, Plattner's account of the furniture of the room was curiously accurate.

One other thing, even at the risk of an irksome repetition, I must insist upon, lest I seem to favour the credulous, superstitious view. Plattner's absence from the world for nine days is, I think, proved. But that does not prove his story. It is quite conceivable that even outside space hallucinations may be possible. That, at least, the reader must bear distinctly in mind.

XVI.

THE RED ROOM.

"I can assure you," said I, "that it will take a very tangible ghost to frighten me." And I stood up before the fire with my glass in my hand.

"It is your own choosing," said the man with the withered arm, and glanced at me askance.

"Eight-and-twenty years," said I, "I have lived, and never a ghost have I seen as yet."

The old woman sat staring hard into the fire, her pale eyes wide open. "Ay," she broke in; "and eight-and-twenty years you have lived and never seen the likes of this house, I reckon. There's a many things to see, when one's still but eight-and-twenty." She swayed her head slowly from side to side. "A many things to see and sorrow for."

I half suspected the old people were trying to enhance the spiritual terrors of their house by their droning insistence. I put down my empty glass on the table and looked about the room, and caught a glimpse of myself, abbreviated and broadened to an impossible sturdiness, in the queer old mirror at the end of the room. "Well," I said, "if I see anything to-night, I shall be so much the wiser. For I come to the business with an open mind."

"It's your own choosing," said the man with the withered arm once more.

I heard the sound of a stick and a shambling step on the flags in the passage outside, and the door creaked on its hinges as a second old man entered, more bent, more wrinkled, more aged even than the first. He supported himself by a single crutch, his eyes were covered by a shade, and his lower lip, half averted, hung pale and pink from his decaying yellow teeth. He made straight for an arm-chair on the opposite side of the table, sat down clumsily, and began to cough. The man with the withered arm gave this new-comer a short glance of positive dislike; the old woman took no notice of his arrival, but remained with her eyes fixed steadily on the fire.

"I said—it's your own choosing," said the man with the withered arm, when the coughing had ceased for a while.

"It's my own choosing," I answered.

The man with the shade became aware of my presence for the first time, and threw his head back for a moment and sideways, to see me. I caught a momentary glimpse of his eyes, small and bright and inflamed. Then he began to cough and splutter again.

"Why don't you drink?" said the man with the withered arm, pushing the beer towards him. The man with the shade poured out a glassful with a shaky hand that splashed half as much again on the deal table. A monstrous shadow of him crouched upon the wall and mocked his action as he poured and drank. I must confess I had scarce expected these grotesque custodians. There is to my mind something inhuman in senility, something crouching and atavistic; the human qualities seem to drop from old people insensibly day by day. The three of them made me feel uncomfortable, with their gaunt silences, their bent carriage, their evident unfriendliness to me and to one another.

"If," said I, "you will show me to this haunted room of yours, I will make myself comfortable there."

The old man with the cough jerked his head back so suddenly that it startled me, and shot another glance of his red eyes at me from under the shade; but no one answered me. I waited a minute, glancing from one to the other.

"If," I said a little louder, "if you will show me to this haunted room of yours, I will relieve you from the task of entertaining me."

"There's a candle on the slab outside the door," said the man with the withered arm, looking at my feet as he addressed me. "But if you go to the red room to-night——"

("This night of all nights!" said the old woman.)

"You go alone."

"Very well," I answered. "And which way do I go?"

"You go along the passage for a bit," said he, "until you come to a door, and through that is a spiral staircase, and half-way up that is a landing and another door covered with baize. Go through that and down the long corridor to the end, and the red room is on your left up the steps."

"Have I got that right?" I said, and repeated his directions. He corrected me in one particular.

"And are you really going?" said the man with the shade, looking at me again for the third time, with that queer, unnatural tilting of the face.

("This night of all nights!" said the old woman.)

"It is what I came for," I said, and moved towards the door. As I did so, the old man with the shade rose and staggered round the table, so as to be closer to the others and to the fire. At the door I turned and looked at them, and saw they were all close together, dark against the firelight, staring at me over their shoulders, with an intent expression on their ancient faces.

"Good-night," I said, setting the door open.

"It's your own choosing," said the man with the withered arm.

I left the door wide open until the candle was well alight, and then I shut them in and walked down the chilly, echoing passage.

I must confess that the oddness of these three old pensioners in whose charge her ladyship had left the castle, and the deep-toned, old-fashioned furniture of the housekeeper's room in which they foregathered, affected me in spite of my efforts to keep myself at a matter-of-fact phase. They seemed to belong to another age, an older age, an age when things spiritual were different from this of ours, less certain; an age when omens and witches were credible, and ghosts beyond denying. Their very existence was spectral; the cut of their clothing, fashions born in dead brains. The ornaments and conveniences of the room about them were ghostly—the thoughts of vanished men, which still haunted rather than participated in the world of to-day. But with an effort I sent such thoughts to the right-about. The long, draughty subterranean passage was chilly and dusty, and my candle flared and made the shadows cower and quiver. The echoes rang up and down the spiral staircase, and a shadow came sweeping up after me, and one fled before me into the darkness overhead. I came to the landing and stopped there for a moment, listening to a rustling that I fancied I heard; then, satisfied of the absolute silence, I pushed open the baize-covered door and stood in the corridor.

The effect was scarcely what I expected, for the moonlight, coming in by the great window on the grand staircase, picked out everything in vivid black shadow or silvery illumination. Everything was in its place: the house might have been deserted on the yesterday instead of eighteen months ago. There were candles in the sockets of the sconces, and whatever dust had gathered on the carpets or upon the polished flooring was distributed so evenly as to be invisible in the moonlight. I was about to advance, and stopped abruptly. A bronze group stood upon the landing, hidden from me by the corner of the wall, but its shadow fell with marvellous distinctness upon the white panelling, and gave me the impression of someone crouching to waylay me. I stood rigid for half a minute perhaps. Then, with my hand in the pocket that held my revolver, I advanced, only to discover a Ganymede and Eagle glistening in the moonlight. That incident for a time restored my nerve, and a porcelain Chinaman on a buhl table, whose head rocked silently as I passed him, scarcely startled me.

The door to the red room and the steps up to it were in a shadowy corner. I moved my candle from side to side, in order to see clearly the nature of the recess in which I stood before opening the door. Here it was, thought I, that my predecessor was found, and the memory of that story gave me a sudden twinge of apprehension. I glanced over my shoulder at the Ganymede in the moonlight, and opened the door of the red room rather hastily, with my face half turned to the pallid silence of the landing.

I entered, closed the door behind me at once, turned the key I found in the lock within, and stood with the candle held aloft, surveying the scene of my vigil, the great red room of Lorraine Castle, in which the young duke had died. Or, rather, in which he had begun his dying, for he had opened the door and fallen headlong down the steps I had just ascended. That had been the end of his vigil, of his gallant attempt to conquer the ghostly tradition of the place, and never, I thought, had apoplexy better served the ends of superstition. And there were other and older stories that clung to the room, back to the half-credible beginning of it all, the tale of a timid wife and the tragic end that came to her husband's jest of frightening her. And looking around that large sombre room, with its shadowy window bays, its recesses and alcoves, one could well understand the legends that had sprouted in its black corners, its germinating darkness. My candle was a little tongue of light in its vastness, that failed to pierce the opposite end of the room, and left an ocean of mystery and suggestion beyond its island of light.

I resolved to make a systematic examination of the place at once, and dispel the fanciful suggestions of its obscurity before they obtained a hold upon me. After satisfying myself of the fastening of the door, I began to walk about the room, peering round each article of furniture, tucking up the valances of the bed, and opening its curtains wide. I pulled up the blinds and examined the fastenings of the several windows before closing the shutters, leant forward and looked up the blackness of the wide chimney, and tapped the dark oak panelling for any secret opening. There were two big mirrors in the room, each with a pair of sconces bearing candles, and on the mantelshelf, too, were more candles in china candlesticks. All these I lit one after the other. The fire was laid, an unexpected consideration from the old housekeeper,—and I lit it, to keep down any disposition to shiver, and when it was burning well, I stood round with my back to it and regarded the room again. I had pulled up a chintz-covered arm-chair and a table, to form a kind of barricade before me, and on this lay my revolver ready to hand. My precise examination had done me good, but I still found the remoter darkness of the place, and its perfect stillness, too stimulating for the imagination. The echoing of the stir and crackling of the fire was no sort of comfort to me. The shadow in the alcove at the end in particular, had that undefinable quality of a presence, that odd suggestion of a lurking, living thing, that comes so easily in silence and solitude. At last, to reassure myself, I walked with a candle into it, and satisfied myself that there was nothing tangible there. I stood that candle upon the floor of the alcove, and left it in that position.

By this time I was in a state of considerable nervous tension, although to my reason there was no adequate cause for the condition. My mind, however, was perfectly clear. I postulated quite unreservedly that nothing supernatural could happen, and to pass the time I began to string some rhymes together, Ingoldsby fashion, of the original legend of the place. A few I spoke aloud, but the echoes were not pleasant. For the same reason I also abandoned, after a time, a conversation with myself upon the impossibility of ghosts and haunting. My mind reverted to the three old and distorted people downstairs, and I tried to keep it upon that topic. The sombre reds and blacks of the room troubled, me; even with seven candles the place was merely dim. The one in the alcove flared in a draught, and the fire-flickering kept the shadows and penumbra perpetually shifting and stirring. Casting about for a remedy, I recalled the candles I had seen in the passage, and, with a slight effort, walked out into the moonlight, carrying a candle and leaving the door open, and presently returned with as many as ten. These I put in various knick-knacks of china with which the room was sparsely adorned, lit and placed where the shadows had lain deepest, some on the floor, some in the window recesses, until at last my seventeen candles were so arranged that not an inch of the room but had the direct light of at least one of them. It occurred to me that when the ghost came, I could warn him not to trip over them. The room was now quite brightly illuminated. There was something very cheery and reassuring in these little streaming flames, and snuffing them gave me an occupation, and afforded a helpful sense of the passage of time. Even with that, however, the brooding expectation of the vigil weighed heavily upon me. It was after midnight that the candle in the alcove suddenly went out, and the black shadow sprang back to its place there. I did not see the candle go out; I simply turned and saw that the darkness was there, as one might start and see the unexpected presence of a stranger. "By Jove!" said I aloud; "that draught's a strong one!" and, taking the matches from the table, I walked across the room in a leisurely manner, to relight the corner again. My first match would not strike, and as I succeeded with the second, something seemed to blink on the wall before me. I turned my head involuntarily, and saw that the two candles on the little table by the fireplace were extinguished. I rose at once to my feet.

"Odd!" I said. "Did I do that myself in a flash of absent-mindedness?"

I walked back, relit one, and as I did so, I saw the candle in the right sconce of one of the mirrors wink and go right out, and almost immediately its companion followed it. There was no mistake about it. The flame vanished, as if the wicks had been suddenly nipped between a finger and a thumb, leaving the wick neither glowing nor smoking, but black. While I stood gaping, the candle at the foot of the bed went out, and the shadows seemed to take another step towards me.

"This won't do!" said I, and first one and then another candle on the mantelshelf followed.

"What's up?" I cried, with a queer high note getting into my voice somehow. At that the candle on the wardrobe went out, and the one I had relit in the alcove followed.

"Steady on!" I said. "These candles are wanted," speaking with a half-hysterical facetiousness, and scratching away at a match the while for the mantel candlesticks. My hands trembled so much that twice I missed the rough paper of the matchbox. As the mantel emerged from darkness again, two candles in the remoter end of the window were eclipsed. But with the same match I also relit the larger mirror candles, and those on the floor near the doorway, so that for the moment I seemed to gain on the extinctions. But then in a volley there vanished four lights at once in different corners of the room, and I struck another match in quivering haste, and stood hesitating whither to take it.

As I stood undecided, an invisible hand seemed to sweep out the two candles on the table. With a cry of terror, I dashed at the alcove, then into the corner, and then into the window, relighting three, as two more vanished by the fireplace; then, perceiving a better way, I dropped the matches on the iron-bound deed-box in the corner, and caught up the bedroom candlestick. With this I avoided the delay of striking matches; but for all that the steady process of extinction went on, and the shadows I feared and fought against returned, and crept in upon me, first a step gained on this side of me and then on that. It was like a ragged storm-cloud sweeping out the stars. Now and then one returned for a minute, and was lost again. I was now almost frantic with the horror of the coming darkness, and my self-possession deserted me. I leaped panting and dishevelled from candle to candle, in a vain struggle against that remorseless advance.

I bruised myself on the thigh against the table, I sent a chair headlong, I stumbled and fell and whisked the cloth from the table in my fall. My candle rolled away from me, and I snatched another as I rose. Abruptly this was blown out, as I swung it off the table by the wind of my sudden movement, and immediately the two remaining candles followed. But there was light still in the room, a red light that staved off the shadows from me. The fire! Of course I could still thrust my candle between the bars and relight it!

I turned to where the flames were still dancing between the glowing coals, and splashing red reflections upon the furniture, made two steps towards the grate, and incontinently the flames dwindled and vanished, the glow vanished, the reflections rushed together and vanished, and as I thrust the candle between the bars darkness closed upon me like the shutting of an eye, wrapped about me in a stifling embrace, sealed my vision, and crushed the last vestiges of reason from my brain. The candle fell from my hand. I flung out my arms in a vain effort to thrust that ponderous blackness away from me, and, lifting up my voice, screamed with all my might—once, twice, thrice. Then I think I must have staggered to my feet. I know I thought suddenly of the moonlit corridor, and, with my head bowed and my arms over my face, made a run for the door.

But I had forgotten the exact position of the door, and struck myself heavily against the corner of the bed. I staggered back, turned, and was either struck or struck myself against some other bulky furniture. I have a vague memory of battering myself thus, to and fro in the darkness, of a cramped struggle, and of my own wild crying as I darted to and fro, of a heavy blow at last upon my forehead, a horrible sensation of falling that lasted an age, of my last frantic effort to keep my footing, and then I remember no more.

I opened my eyes in daylight. My head was roughly bandaged, and the man with the withered arm was watching my face. I looked about me, trying to remember what had happened, and for a space I could not recollect. I rolled my eyes into the corner, and saw the old woman, no longer abstracted, pouring out some drops of medicine from a little blue phial into a glass. "Where am I?" I asked; "I seem to remember you, and yet I cannot remember who you are."

They told me then, and I heard of the haunted Red Room as one who hears a tale. "We found you at dawn," said he, "and there was blood on your forehead and lips."

It was very slowly I recovered my memory of my experience. "You believe now," said the old man, "that the room is haunted?" He spoke no longer as one who greets an intruder, but as one who grieves for a broken friend.

"Yes," said I; "the room is haunted."

"And you have seen it. And we, who have lived here all our lives, have never set eyes upon it. Because we have never dared... Tell us, is it truly the old earl who——"

"No," said I; "it is not."

"I told you so," said the old lady, with the glass in her hand. "It is his poor young countess who was frightened——"

"It is not," I said. "There is neither ghost of earl nor ghost of countess in that room, there is no ghost there at all; but worse, far worse——"

"Well?" they said.

"The worst of all the things that haunt poor mortal man," said I; "and that is, in all its nakedness—Fear that will not have light nor sound, that will not bear with reason, that deafens and darkens and overwhelms. It followed me through the corridor, it fought against me in the room——"

I stopped abruptly. There was an interval of silence. My hand went up to my bandages.

Then the man with the shade sighed and spoke. "That is it," said he. "I knew that was it. A power of darkness. To put such a curse upon a woman! It lurks there always. You can feel it even in the daytime, even of a bright summer's day, in the hangings, in the curtains, keeping behind you however you face about. In the dusk it creeps along the corridor and follows you, so that you dare not turn. There is Fear in that room of hers—black Fear, and there will be—so long as this house of sin endures."

XVII.

THE PURPLE PILEUS

Mr. Coombes was sick of life. He walked away from his unhappy home, and, sick not only of his own existence but of everybody else's, turned aside down Gaswork Lane to avoid the town, and, crossing the wooden bridge that goes over the canal to Starling's Cottages, was presently alone in the damp pine woods and out of sight and sound of human habitation. He would stand it no longer. He repeated aloud with blasphemies unusual to him that he would stand it no longer.

He was a pale-faced little man, with dark eyes and a fine and very black moustache. He had a very stiff, upright collar slightly frayed, that gave him an illusory double chin, and his overcoat (albeit shabby) was trimmed with astrachan. His gloves were a bright brown with black stripes over the knuckles, and split at the finger ends. His appearance, his wife had said once in the dear, dead days beyond recall—before he married her, that is—was military. But now she called him—it seems a dreadful thing to tell of between husband and wife, but she called him "a little grub." It wasn't the only thing she had called him, either.

The row had arisen about that beastly Jennie again. Jennie was his wife's friend, and, by no invitation of Mr. Coombes, she came in every blessed Sunday to dinner, and made a shindy all the afternoon. She was a big, noisy girl, with a taste for loud colours and a strident laugh; and this Sunday she had outdone all her previous intrusions by bringing in a fellow with her, a chap as showy as herself. And Mr. Coombes, in a starchy, clean collar and his Sunday frock-coat, had sat dumb and wrathful at his own table, while his wife and her guests talked foolishly and undesirably, and laughed aloud. Well, he stood that, and after dinner (which, "as usual," was late), what must Miss Jennie do but go to the piano and play banjo tunes, for all the world as if it were a week-day! Flesh and blood could not endure such goings on. They would hear next door, they would hear in the road, it was a public announcement of their disrepute. He had to speak.

He had felt himself go pale, and a kind of rigour had affected his respiration as he delivered himself. He had been sitting on one of the chairs by the window—the new guest had taken possession of the arm-chair. He turned his head. "Sun Day!" he said over the collar, in the voice of one who warns. "Sun Day!" What people call a "nasty" tone, it was.

Jennie had kept on playing, but his wife, who was looking through some music that was piled on the top of the piano, had stared at him. "What's wrong now?" she said; "can't people enjoy themselves?"

"I don't mind rational 'njoyment, at all," said little Coombes, "but I ain't a-going to have week-day tunes playing on a Sunday in this house."

"What's wrong with my playing now?" said Jennie, stopping and twirling round on the music-stool with a monstrous rustle of flounces.

Coombes saw it was going to be a row, and opened too vigorously, as is common with your timid, nervous men all the world over. "Steady on with that music-stool!" said he; "it ain't made for 'eavy-weights."

"Never you mind about weights," said Jennie, incensed. "What was you saying behind my back about my playing?"

"Surely you don't 'old with not having a bit of music on a Sunday, Mr. Coombes?" said the new guest, leaning back in the arm-chair, blowing a cloud of cigarette smoke and smiling in a kind of pitying way. And simultaneously his wife said something to Jennie about "Never mind 'im. You go on, Jinny."

"I do," said Mr. Coombes, addressing the new guest.

"May I arst why?" said the new guest, evidently enjoying both his cigarette and the prospect of an argument. He was, by-the-by, a lank young man, very stylishly dressed in bright drab, with a white cravat and a pearl and silver pin. It had been better taste to come in a black coat, Mr. Coombes thought.

"Because," began Mr. Coombes, "it don't suit me. I'm a business man. I 'ave to study my connection. Rational 'njoyment—"

"His connection!" said Mrs. Coombes scornfully. "That's what he's always a-saying. We got to do this, and we got to do that—"

"If you don't mean to study my connection," said Mr. Coombes, "what did you marry me for?"

"I wonder," said Jennie, and turned back to the piano.

"I never saw such a man as you," said Mrs. Coombes.

"You've altered all round since we were

Made in the USA
Monee, IL
06 December 2022

19784735R00125